THE LAST
KINGS

A STORY BY
C.N. PHILLIPS

THE LAST KINGS

Book Layout: Oddball Dsgn
Cover Design: Oddball Dsgn

For further information log onto www.ashleyjaquavis.com

Printed in the United States

♟ PROLOGUE

MOCHA

To me motivation was just another word with a dictionary meaning. A meaning that didn't pertain to me anymore. I stood in the mirror of a sleazy hotel bathroom staring into the dirty mirror above the sink. Staring back was a woman with wide light brown eyes that might have been pretty had it not been for the smeared mascara and bags under them. The long black hair, once neatly in place, was now disheveled. The red lipstick on my lips faded. I could barely recognize myself.

What am I doing? I thought to myself and grabbed a handful of my hair.

I stood there in my matching black lace lingeric set; the sexiest that I could afford. The curves on my twenty-two year old body stood out, and although tired the beauty in my round face did too. I heard my client snore lightly in the other room. I always put them to sleep that way it was easier to collect my money and sneak out the door. That night was different though. I wanted to look at myself. Not just look, actually *see* myself. In the act, not the aftermath of designer shoes, clothes and purses. So after I was done with my client that was exactly what I did. I looked at the bitch in the mirror and hated her. I hated me.

I reached and grabbed a cigarette out of the box of Newport's my client left on the sink in the bathroom and the lighter next to them; my body needed something to stomach my reflection. It was sad seeing myself like that, especially knowing that at one point in time I was on top of shit. Although my appearance was disgraceful I knew one thing, I was going to go collect my money. I took a few hits of the cigarette before putting it out on the sink, leaving a circle burn mark. I didn't give a fuck. It wasn't my bill. I then quietly opened the bathroom door and tiptoed to the end of the bed where my cream colored mini dress lay. I put it on as quickly as I could and slipped my tall black pumps on my feet. My money had been left on the dresser; I had to see my money up front. Two thousand dollars for one night with Mocha. I looked disgustedly at the plump white man laying on the motel bed before grabbing my Gucci and my money. I didn't know how much longer I could do this. I exited the room feeling like even less of a woman than any of the other times. I walked a little way to my all black 2011 Chevy Impala SS. Getting in I was relieved to finally be on my way home, even though that wasn't any better than that nasty hotel. Still, laying in *my* bed sounded good.

I was what some called a prostitute or whore. I hated those names, but it was what it was. What I did was dangerous, but my clientele weren't just random thugs off of the streets of Detroit. They were rich men, some married and others just lonely. The guy that night usually took me to high class pent houses and suites but that night he wanted to try a different fantasy. He wanted to fuck me in a cheap hotel like the dirty little black whore I was. Whatever, as long as he was paying me. My money was top priority. Two thousand only got my clients an hour. Only sex if they didn't drop an additional two more stacks on top of the hourly rate, as you can see he was one of my lower paying customers.

It didn't take that long to get to my shabby neighborhood and surprisingly the streets of Detroit were silent that night. I rode with my windows slightly cracked. No music just me and my thoughts. I drove by a few niggas patrolling the block ready to make a sale if need be. I missed that life. The fast money lifestyle with no dignity lost. I guess there was that little spec of hustler still in me although it had subsided over the last year since the murder of my best friend. Since I'd been out of the game a lot had changed; for one I'd become a prostitute and the quick money and respect I was used to faded. I think I hated myself so much because I didn't know how to make it without her. She had been the leader since we were kids, the master mind in all that we did and I missed her.

We were freshman at a local college when we figured out that what we wanted school couldn't give us, never ending money and power. At first a drug cartel was just a little joke between us, but then Sadie's big cousin Ray came to us on some Ace Boogie type shit. Ray came across an Italian connect by the name of Vinny. He could provide never ending business. An Italian man named Vinny. Sadie was down instantly, but I was a little skeptical. Sadie of course talked me into it and before I knew it we were getting it in big time. It was scary at first, being a girl in the game was like a person swimming in a pool full of hungry sharks. But we started off big time, so it wasn't hard maintaining a leveled spot where the top began. Ray then got us our first pistols.

"Niggas hate seeing a come up," he said. "Especially when they're looking for one."

His words held true because less than a week later I had to use my .48 that I'd named Lucy for the first time. Somebody had got wind to our operation on the come up, and had set us up. That night I killed somebody, shit I think I killed a few people. That's when I officially said fuck it. One way in, and one way out was how Sadie and I saw it, we were about that life as soon as we had made our first sale. It was money over everything in the beginning. The money rolled in and our team got larger. In less than a year we had the biggest drug operation Detroit had ever seen, nobody was touching us. Not even the feds. Our shit was so underground they didn't know who to trail. Sadie and I dropped out of school when we were twenty and moved in with Ray. Shit was doing great until I did the dumbest shit somebody in my seat of power could do. I fell in love. Like Ray said, niggas are always looking for a come up. But I was too blinded by my heart that I didn't see what Khiron was doing until it was too late. Until he got what he really wanted; to be on top and to control our empire. He wanted everything Sadie and I had worked for and unlike the boss that I was supposed to be, I was caught slipping.

Another thing Ray was known for saying was, *"All your niggas ain't loyal."*

The Last Kings was betrayed by someone who should have been their most loyal. I remember seeing

Khiron's bullet enter Sadie's body...seeing her choke on her own blood until she died. Right there in front of me. Ray was next.

"You, Mocha, aren't going to get the luxury of death," Khy had said to me.

I would never forget those words. Every day after that I wished he would just kill me. Most nights I came home and he was there waiting for me. I was his trophy piece. His way of showing he'd brought down the best. He was the king of our cartel, nobody was fucking with him. Little did he know his plan was flawed. He hadn't thought it through completely.

See Ray had been planning on getting out of the game. Calling it quits, he had enough money stacked up. He'd told one of us the information about his connect and that one wasn't me. Surprise, surprise. That put a slight dent in Khy's plan especially when the Italians pulled business and went ghost but Khy had his own connect and so far the streets were taken care of. Khy was a demon, I hated him. I sold my body at night just so I could stack up my paper and get away from him. Far away. There was nothing left in Detroit for me. He had taken it all.

He moved me back into the hood to keep an eye on me while he lived like royalty in a mansion on the good side of town. I had a nice car, nobody bothered me, he paid all of my bills, and I didn't have any worries. That's what he told me constantly. He wouldn't even let me go back to school and get a semi fresh start.

"Bitches like you belong at home in the kitchen or on their knees for they man," he said when I brought the subject up.

Khy changed from the man that I first knew. I take that back, I never knew that son of a bitch, I met that nigga's game face. I knew him now though, and he had hell to pay. Coming up on my home, I slowed to turn into the driveway of my one story brick house. A shadow on my stoop caught my eye and I could see that there was a person posted up, as if they were waiting.

"Who the fuck is that?" I said aloud to myself unbuckling my seatbelt.

It couldn't have been Khy, he had a key. The person stood up when I opened my door and it was dark out but I could make out the frame of a woman. At first I thought she must be a crack head looking for a hit but the closer I got I knew she couldn't have been. She was in designer clothes and heels.

"Excuse me, but who the fuck are you?" I asked bluntly putting my hand in my purse.

I wasn't scared, Lucy was in my Gucci loaded and ready to bust. The stranger stepped down the three steps from my stoop towards the light by my garage door. Her features became more distinguished as the shadows no longer concealed her. I opened my mouth to speak again, but I caught my breath and my heart became a drummer in my chest. The woman before me looked different than I remembered; her hair was in a bob cut. But the sharpness in her dark brown eyes were the same and she was still gorgeous with her five-five frame and coca-cola shape. I couldn't believe it. I took a deep breath.

"Sadie?"

C.N. PHILLIPS

THREE YEARS EARLIER

♟ CHAPTER 1

"**M**ocha wake your lazy ass up!" I yelled at my best friend who was snoozing loudly in her bed.

She continued snoring and like she hadn't heard me, although I'm pretty sure the people in the dorm next to us had. I grabbed a pillow from my bed and hauled it across the room at her. It hit her dead in her pretty sleeping face. The expression it held when she was fully awake almost made me regret my actions.

"The fuck Sadie!" Mocha sat up and shot me the dirtiest look she could muster.

I laughed, I couldn't help it. Who could take a person seriously when they had slobber sliding down their face. Not to mention her hair was all over the place.

"Shut up bitch and go clean yourself up, we have class in an hour." I said back to her still grinning.

"I don't see anything funny! I was sleeping good!" Mocha said stretching.

"Clearly," I said sarcastically.

"Fuck you Sadie I'm not going to class. I'm tired," Mocha tried to throw the covers back over her.

"Well if you weren't out fucking Antwan's ass all night you wouldn't be tired!" I walked to her side of our dorm and snatched the cover back. "Your hoe ass should have remembered you had class in the morning."

Antwan was Mocha's newest male interest. He was a wanna be hustler who thought he was the shit, key word, thought. I personally didn't see what she saw in his tall black ass; besides his perfect smile and smooth chocolate skin. I saw nothing appealing about him. He attended a few classes at the community college in Detroit, Michigan that Mocha and I attended and he must have laid the D on her something vicious. He had my girl's head gone.

"Girl don't hate!" Mocha said sitting up. "Just because your pussy is covered in cobwebs doesn't mean you have to rain on my parade!"

I rolled my eyes at her comment. She was completely wrong and I let her know so.

"Bitch, my pussy has standards unlike yours. Mrs. Bust It Wide Open for anyone with a big dick," I threw some clothes at her. "And don't forget that the only reason we're even here is because of our scholarships, we don't have time to slack off. I even picked out your outfit!"

I was already dressed in a Victoria Secrets Pink hoodie and sweats; except they were purple with my light tan Uggs. My long dark brown hair was pulled on the top of my head in a bun. I had picked out a similar out fit for Mocha; except hers was red. I loved how the pants insinuated the curves of our hips and plumpness of our behinds.

"I fucking hate your ass," Mocha stood up with her clothes and headed for the bathroom.

I could tell she had just recently fucked by the way she was walking, yet trying to pretend her legs weren't sore, "You got forty-five minutes!" I yelled as the bathroom door slammed shut. Twenty minutes later Mocha walked out of the bathroom looking like a shapely model. I had always been a little jealous of Mocha's figure. We both had curves for days, but her ass was a little pumper than mine and her hips a little wider. I got more luck than her in the chest department with my 36-C sized breasts; she couldn't even fit a C. Her creamy mocha latte colored skin was silky smooth. She wore her long hair wet crinkled but pulled back in a tight ponytail. The ponytail brought out the light green specks in her light brown eyes.

"Awe boo!" I gushed at her natural beauty.

"Leave me alone Sadie, I'm still pissed off at you," she was trying hard to hold back her grin.

"Whatever," I handed her designer Coach backpack to her. "Let's go before we're late."

Mocha put on her matching Uggs and we grabbed our coats. I locked our room up and we were on our way. I made small talk on our way to our math class, mainly to keep my mind off of the cold nipping away at my ears.

"Have you talked to Ray?" I asked Mocha swerving to miss a young white guy riding his bike on the tiny campus.

"Bitch he's your cousin," Mocha shivered as she walked. "You would hear from him before I would!"

I rolled my eyes at her smart remark, mainly because it held truth to it. Although my grandma had taken Mocha in at the age of fifteen after her dad was murdered and her mom ran off with the first man who would take her, she wasn't my blood. Ray looked at her like his little cousin, but we were closer. It hadn't felt like it the last three or four months though. It seemed like he was distant. He set Mocha and I up with everything designer kept our pockets full, but that still didn't make up for the absence of my favorite cousin. I knew that his name was loud in the streets and I knew what he did to keep it that way. Ray seemed to always be busy; with my school schedule I barely saw him.

We had almost made it to the building our class was in when we heard a deep voice and foot steps behind us.

"God knows he's wrong for giving' y'all all that ass!"

I whipped my head around ready to curse whoever it was out. I calmed down when I saw it was nobody but Antwan's black ass.

"You're so stupid," I shot him a dirty look.

"Antwan it's too early," Mocha tried to sound annoyed but I could tell she was a little happy at just the sight of him.

I couldn't lie, Antwan was looking fresh with his hair newly cut and was rocking Ralph Lauren head to toe. But still he was so not my type. He licked his lips hungrily at Mocha.

"Yeah it is too early," Antwan caught up to us and began walking in between us. "What are the two baddest bitches on campus even dong up right now?"

"I'm not a bitch," Mocha snapped. "And we have class silly, this is a school. Why the fuck else would we be up?"

Antwan chuckled and shook his head.

"Yeah this is a school, and you obviously didn't check the school website either. If you're not an upcoming graduate you ain't got school all week. Something about neighborhood violence or some shit."

Mocha stopped in her tracks and glared at me.

"Fuck!" I said remembering I had seen that the night before. "I forgot!"

"Fuck is right! Because I'ma fuck you up!" Mocha told me.

"Damn, I said sorry!"

"When? I didn't hear it!" Mocha huffed.

I wanted to punch her, but she was right. It was my mistake.

Antwan was cracking up.

"Aye man, you two are a trip! I'm going to fuck with y'all later though," Antwan said and continued walking.

"Where are you going?" Mocha inquired.

"I got some business to handle," he said. "Aye Sadie?"

"What's up?" I asked wondering what on Earth he could have to say to me.

"My man C.J. wants to know what's up with you?"

"Not a damn thing!" I informed him sternly.

C.J. was Antwan's best friend who Mocha talked me into going out with. Whereas C.J was sexier than a muhfucka and had a big dick to back it up. After a few dates and him discussing nothing but himself and money I just couldn't do it. Also after our third date I actually let him come into my dorm so we could get it in. His ass couldn't even last two minutes, and we tried two times. I stopped answering his calls after that, and he hadn't stopped trying to get at me. It made me mad because I didn't give myself to many people and when I did it usually was worth it.

"Damn! It's like that?" Antwan laughed loudly.

"Yeah it's like that! Tell him when he can last longer than two minutes his bitch ass *still* won't have a chance with me!"

"Alright I feel you ma," he said and gave us two fingers to tell us goodbye.

"I cannot believe your ass has me out in the cold and we don't even have class!" Mocha kept saying the whole way back to our dorm room. Once there she climbed right back into her bed after throwing off her coat and shoes.

I sat down on my colorful polka dotted comforter and looked at my best friend.

"I'm sorry Mocha; you know I wouldn't have woke your crazy ass up if I would have remembered we didn't have class today. That was a waste of both of our time."

"Fuck that, even if we did you shouldn't have woke me up. I'm tired of this shit," she said snuggling back under her covers.

I knew exactly what she meant. About a week ago Mocha and I had a discussion after her school trip to Atlanta on the reason why we were in school in the first place. What we wanted to be when we graduated. Neither of us had an answer. We both made good grades. But we both had always hated school. If it hadn't been for my Grandma Rae we probably would have dropped out as soon as we could have. We lucked up and got scholarships at the community college in Detroit.

Grandma Rae made us go. and we only stayed because of the fat refund checks we got every semester. Mocha was a math genius, like Ray, and I excelled in English. Fuck that. That night we talked about using our refund check money to start our own little business, Mocha had jokingly said something about starting a drug cartel. It was crazy because with all of the knowledge I had about it, I never thought about getting into the game myself. Mainly because every single one of the men my mother dated were hustlers who met sticky endings. No matter how much of a boss they were. Also one of the worst experiences in my life that I would forever live with happened due to that game, and the life that came with it. I was skeptical about that idea. If it came down to it though I know I would be down for the ride.

"Real shit Mocha, I feel you," I said laying back on my bed. "This shit is getting played out to me too. If I didn't think Grandma Rae would flip I would have been gone."

"I know. These petty ass refund checks can't cover the kind of taste I have. I'm tired of Ray buying all of our shit. One day he isn't going to be here, and school isn't taking me anywhere. I need to figure out what I'm going to do with my life. Right now I feel as if I'm wasting it taking tests that aren't going to fill my pockets with that green shit."

"We can get jobs," I said but instantly took it back. I couldn't picture either of us flipping anyone's burgers. "Nevermind."

"Right, the working world ain't for us," Mocha agreed turning to face my bed.

"Yeah," I agreed.

There were a few minutes of silence before Mocha began speaking, a little more quiet that time.

"So you haven't talked to Ray at all?"

"No," I told her. "I don't know what's been up with us lately. I used to talk to him every day."

"Yeah you know what they're saying right? About Coopa's shit?"

I nodded my head. Coopa was the king pin of Detroit. He kept his shit tight. From what I heard and seen was a nigga you didn't want to fuck with. He shot first and didn't ask or answer any questions. He was a good looking man in his late thirties; light skin with small brown eyes and well respected in the game. He currently was the head of the biggest drug trafficking operation the city of Detroit had ever seen, and his team consisted of all the hustlers in Detroit. Ray was like his right hand man. Which meant that meant Ray was big. Lately I had been hearing that some niggas wanted Coopa's head on a stick, he had been making some business deals and not holding up his end of the bargain. He thought he was untouchable, and so far he had been. I just didn't want Ray in any shit because of Coopa's business dealings.

"What do you think about it?" Mocha asked me.

"I mean what can I say? Ray's a grown ass man. I just hope that when Coopa goes down, Ray doesn't either," I told her.

"Maybe he was waiting for the right time to get out," Mocha threw out.

"Nah, Ray loves his life too much. If anything he would just take over. Then we could finally drop out of this bitch," I said.

"What does that mean?" Mocha asked.

"Nothing," I said not really knowing what I was saying.

"Sadie, are you really thinking about that?" Mocha asked. "I thought we were just playing around with that shit."

"That 'shit' would be better than just sitting here wasting my life away doing nothing," I told her.

"You tripping, you're trying to be on some crazy shit," Mocha said.

"Some Ashley Antoinette type shit," I said glancing at my book shelf.

"Ok Say," Mocha said calling me by my nickname. "This isn't a book! This is real life! Let's be real for a second. If we start up our own shit it would get shut down before we even took flight! Antwan told me about what Coopa did to those niggas from California. Their bodies were found in dumpsters. Fuck with that shit if you want to Sadie, but it's not smart. What makes it worse is that we're females!"

Mocha's rant went in one ear and out the other. I wasn't scared of Coopa, he was a nigga who stood behind his army instead of in the front. Fuck him. It kind of pissed me off that Ray was working with a snake.

"Whatever Mocha," I didn't feel like arguing with her especially since she had been the one to even bring it up.

"For real Sadie, do you think they would take us seriously?" She asked. "I mean we don't know shit about the game to even try to play."

"*You* don't know shit about the game Mocha," I said and I thought about the question.

I knew the city was hungry but I also knew that even though Copa was running shit. He wasn't handling business like he should have been. Eventually Detroit would birth a new king, so why not make it a queen?

"I don't know, Mocha. Maybe, but only if we were strapped heavy and had a team of loyal riders," I finally answered.

Mocha sighed heavily.

"I'm going to sleep. Your ass is crazy."

I heard her turn over and I lay facing the ceiling for a few more moments with my own personal thoughts. If I could come up with a way to take the dope game by storm, I'd do it in a second. I grew up around it, the attraction I had to it was impossible to ignore. It was undeniable. Since the age of ten when my mother started messing with hustlers it intrigued me. It was also one of the reasons my Grandma Rae ended up with custody of me. I remembered my mom had a new man almost every six months who gave into all of her lavish wants and needs. My mother wasn't just your typical beauty, she was drop dead gorgeous. Her father was part Dominican so her hair flowed almost to her butt. She didn't believe in the working world. She played off of her wide hips and plump breasts and it worked for her. We moved around a lot, and in every city she would date the new "big thing," until he either got himself killed or incarcerated. The longest relationship was for two years and I hated him. His name was Nino and I was fourteen at the time. I was just coming into my looks and many would often tell me I was beautiful just like my mother. My mother moved us into his large six bedroom estate and promised me that "this was it." Like a fool I believed her. It didn't take long for the fairy tale dream to be shattered. Nino was an angry and possessive woman beater. Whenever my mother did anything he didn't agree with he would floor her. For a while my mother put up with it saying that she needed him and if it weren't for him we would be on the streets. But when Nino started paying attention to me things started to really get out of control. Instead of protecting me like a mother should have my mother turned to drugs. The same ones Nino was selling to the crack whores roaming the streets. The first night Nino raped me he put a gun to my head and told me if I screamed he would blow me and my mother's heads off.

I had never felt pain like that before in my fourteen years and I felt lower than dirt. He was large, too large for a girl's first time. I remember biting my lip so I wouldn't scream. My womanhood was stripped from me in thirty minutes and fifteen seconds. I knew that because I'd closed my eyes and counted to evade Nino as he humped my body deeper and deeper into the mattress. No matter how much of a failure my mother was she was still my mother and I didn't want him to hurt her any more than he already had. After that first time it began happening periodically. I never spoke a word of it to my mother. Whenever she looked at me her eyes reeked with sadness and pain. I knew she knew and the fact that she didn't do anything to stop it hurt. My mother had completely lost her shape and any beauty once in her face was gone. Nino actually began using me to make drops and collect his money. I used to take the drugs to school. When my beeper went off I knew a customer was out front. Not the smartest idea in the books but I never got caught so it worked for me.

Nino had a son that lived with his mother but he flew out often to see him leaving my mother and me at peace. I remembered the last time he flew out to see him was the day after he had raped me so brutally that I bled all over the sheets. I decided then that I wasn't going to spend the rest of my life as his sex slave and flunky so I snuck into his. I knew I could find something in there to get him caught up. Sure enough I did. It seemed that Nino, much like Coopa, had been making some bad business moves and owed a few people money. I made a few calls with the numbers I found and when I was done all I had to do was play the waiting game. It didn't happen right away but I knew it wouldn't. I had a few more horrible nights when Nino came back, but it was all worth it as soon as I heard the front door being kicked in. At the time my mother and I were in the kitchen eating our dinner. When my mother heard the door cave in she grabbed me and made a dash to the upstairs part of the house.

"What the fuck Camara?" Nino screamed at my mother when we burst into the room they shared.

"They found us," my mom said in a hurried hushed tone. "We have to go, now!"

Nino jumped up grabbing his gun and ran to shut the door behind us. I could tell by the look in his eyes that he was terrified. We heard the people under us ransacking the house and knew it would only be a matter of time before they found us.

"*But how did they find me?*" Nino asked himself trying to think of how they found his house. His house wasn't even listed; he had done that as a safety precaution knowing his head was wanted on a few sticks. His eyes then locked with mine and I couldn't help the devilish upward curl that formed on my mouth. "It was you!"

Before he could grab me the door flung open and shots rang out in the room. I will never forget seeing the shots rain into Nino's body. That was the last sight I saw before my mother grabbed me and we fell back into the tall bookcase. In a matter of seconds we were in another room. My mother was frantically grabbing already packed suitcases and stacks of money. I had never seen my mom move that fast. I remember hearing them yelling about fucking with "The Boss's" money and how they trusted him with the coke. Instead he was snorting it with a bitch. There was a window in the room and my mother told me to climb out it and use the side railing to slide down to the ground. I heard one final gun shot and my mother pushed me out of the window. Once we were both on the ground we ran as fast as we could to her car and as we drove away from the house I looked behind me only to see the beginning of it being burned to the ground. We drove all the way to Grandma Rae's house where she left dropped me off saying she needed to grab a few things. But never came back. I guess that's another reason why Mocha and I were so close. We were both abandoned by our mothers. I never told her the full story, no one knew.

Finally I decided to put my thoughts to the back of my mind and get a few more hours of sleep. I turned the lamp beside my bed off and let my thoughts consume me until I fell asleep.

♟ CHAPTER 2

I woke up to the sound of my phone ringing next to my head on my white fluffy pillow. I wasn't quick to answer it; I was wondering who the hell was calling me.

"Hello?" My voice sounded groggy.

"What up!" I recognized the deep voice. The one and only Ray. "I know your ass isn't still sleep at one o clock?"

"Don't what up me!" I said suddenly wide awake. "Where the fuck have you been?"

"Chill! Get up I'm about to pull up in five minutes. Tell Mocha to get up too. I know her ass is still passed out if you are."

I looked over to Mocha, whose mouth was hanging open. I laughed a little bit.

"I'm assuming that I'm right," Ray said.

"Shut up Ray, you better have your gloves because when I see you I'm beating your ass. Especially with the shit I've been hearing."

"Yeah yeah, I'm here, come out."

I hung up then proceeded to wake Mocha up.

"Mocha get up, Ray's here," I shook her arm.

"Sadie I am going to fuck you up! This is the second time you've fucked up my beauty sleep!" Mocha tried to swat me off of her but I didn't let her arm go.

"Ray is outside, get up!"

"I wish you would just leave me aloooone!" she grumbled putting on her boots and coat.

"Shut up, I know you don't want to be cooped in this small ass dorm room all day," I said trying to hurry and get out to the car.

Even though I was mad at him I was excited to see my cousin. It had been too long. The money he sent us every week didn't make up for his absence. I'm glad Mocha and I were still dressed from earlier because it didn't take too long to get out of our dorm.

"Lock the door behind you," I told Mocha.

"*Nah*, I'm just going to leave it unlocked," she said sarcastically and locked the door. "Why is he picking us up?"

"I don't know," I answered honestly going down the one flight of stairs and once again out into the cold air.

I saw his black Cadillac Escalade parked not too far from the dorm's entrance and lead the way avoiding big piles of snow. His tint was so dark I could barely see inside of the car.

"What's up?" Ray grinned at us.

"Hey cousin!" I grinned right on back getting in the passenger seat. I couldn't help it, Ray was so handsome and his smile was contagious.

He had his long dreads hanging and I could see his little goatee trying to come in on his chestnut brown face. He was casual wearing a Diamond Supply T-shirt and 501 Levi jeans. On his feet he wore his French Blue 13's. My cousin was fresh when he wasn't; I couldn't help but to smile. His dark brown eyes were identical to mine except his were sharper when looked into. He looked just like our Grandma Rae, which was why my uncle Thomas named him Raymond. Ray was handsome, and built. He had bitches falling at his feet but he was paying too much attention to his money to take notice. To his enemies Ray was lethal. He held his temper real well, but you definitely didn't want to get on his bad side. He showed mad love to those he cared about. He was the big brother I never had.

"Ray," Mocha said hopping into the backseat, "You better take us to get something to eat!"

Ray gave Mocha the side eye.

"What were you doing still even sleep, it's the afternoon. New better question why the fuck weren't y'all in class?" He took his eyes off of the road to glance at me.

"Damn!" I exclaimed. "Feds ass nigga! We didn't have class today. Check him out Mocha. He's worried about our schooling but we haven't even heard from his ass. "

"Right!" Mocha cosigned laughing.

"Yea laugh if ya' want to but don't try and turn this around on me Sadie," Ray said. "You both know it would fuck with Grandma Rae's heart if she found out y'all were fucking off in school."

"Fuck school! I'm about sick and tired of this shit!" Mocha said in an exasperated tone. "Grandma Rae just might have to be mad at me, because I'm about to throw in the towel after this semester."

"Me too," I agreed.

Ray shook his head at us.

"Y'all tripping. You both saw how pissed Grandma Rae was when she found out I had dropped out of college," Ray reminded us.

He was right; I had never seen Grandma Rae that upset. But at the end of the day it was what it was. No one forced her to go or stay in school, so why should I be forced to?

"Nigga I just want to be on, fuck college" I said.

"Fuck college huh?" Ray chuckled. "I feel you though."

"Yup. You should feel me because you're living' the life. I just don't know why you hitting the block for a nigga that's losing to the game. The streets are talking."

"I don't work for Coopa, I work with Coopa. Fuck what the streets are saying. This is a business, and the only people who really know what the fuck is going on are the people *in* the business. Period."

I rolled my eyes in a "Whatever," like fashion and looked out my window before the conversation went on any further. I noticed we reached a restaurant a few blocks away from Grandma Rae's house that I never even knew was there.

"Roll your eyes at me again and in a second you're going to be looking' like Beyoncé when that bitch fell down them fuckin' stairs!"

I tried not to, but I started cracking up thinking back to when I'd first seen the video. I loved me some Beyoncé, but only a person without eyes wouldn't think that fall was hilarious. I heard Mocha's high pitch laugh join mine.

"Fuck you Ray!" I said opening my door. "You can't park for shit!" I noticed that he was slightly over the line in his slot.

Ray lead the way to the little farm house shaped restaurant. Once inside the host led us to our seats telling us our server would be right with us. We took off our coats and got comfortable in our seats.

"How are your cars running?" He asked us.

Ray had also purchased Mocha and me matching BMW 128i coupes. Mine white, hers all black. Nothing too flashy; just something to get us from point A to point B.

"They're good; I'm ready to be sitting on something big like you though!" Mocha beamed.

It was well known that Ray had an array of vehicles. All paid for. He would always say he wasn't a predictable nigga. When he pulled up most times you wouldn't even know, but his truck was his baby. It was decked out with everything luxury and the complete outer layer was bullet proof.

Ray laughed, "Nah y'all straight. Niggas like me need more than one car."

In that one statement he separated himself from the two of us. My cousin was paid, period. He recycled cars like girls recycled panties.

"Bullshit," Mocha waived her hand at him. "A sexy girl needs a sexy car. One she can get around in the snow in!"

"Nah Mocha, you just can't drive don't blame the car," I joked and she threw a balled up napkin at me.

"You two haven't been out here much have you?" Ray asked changing the subject.

"And if we were I'm sure you would already know," I gave him a smug look. It was hard having a life when your big cousin knew damn near the whole city. Even if he hadn't seen us in forever he would know about our whereabouts. Ray tried to give us some kind of independence after high school. After we complained about having his goons with us at all times. But I knew that he never really gave in to that, he just made his goons unseen to our eyes.

"You're really like the fuckin feds Ray," Mocha shook her head. "Can't even get my cat scratched without your ass all up in my shit!"

The look on Ray's face said he wanted to reach across the table a wring her neck, but he was cool. Mocha and I were the only ones besides Grandma Rae and Ray's best friend Tyler who spoke their minds to Ray, but we knew when to shut up. At the age of twenty four Ray was the type of man that when he got mad, you ducked. With his 6'2 frame and muscular build I could see why many were intimidated by him. He set off the aura of a no bullshit type of nigga. Another thing about Ray that I admired was that no matter what he was wearing he always carried the essence of a Boss, such as that very moment. Eyes kept shifting to and from our table, everyone knew who he was but no one tried to approach.

Ray was actually very educated and could hold a conversation with anyone about anything. Grandma Rae was upset about him dropping out of school, but she stood by his decision. She knew what Ray was doing, but what could she do? Ray was a grown ass man in his own big ass house. If Mocha and I followed in his footsteps I knew it would break her heart. She wanted me to be some amazing doctor or some shit but I knew that wasn't me. I eyed Ray from my side of the table gathering my thoughts.

"How'd you find this place?" Mocha asked looking around the restaurant.

The place was called All Or Nothing, and it was packed with people. The aroma was wonderful and the design was very high end and classy. There were red booths against the walls of the square shaped restaurant and black tables with red chairs in the middle. On the walls there were replicas of famous framed paintings and all of the help wore white collared shirts, black pants, and red bow ties. I was completely unaware of such a nice restaurant in a bad neighborhood.

"I know the owner," Ray shrugged. "I gave him a little something to start the place and ever since whenever I come in he hooks me up."

"Nigga you know everybody!" Mocha shook her head.

"It's called networking, try it sometime," Ray said just as our waitress came to take our orders. "Speaking of which, Mocha, how was your trip to Atlanta?"

Mocha looked slightly caught off guard but she caught herself.

"It was ok, it's not like I was there on vacation. We went to some bullshit ass museum and looked at some dead muhfucka's remains," she mumbled not really looking at him.

I couldn't help wondering why she was acting so strange. Mocha didn't really speak about the trip to Atlanta she'd taken with her Anatomy class; I just figured it must have been boring and she didn't want to dwell on it. Mocha's face spelled relief when a pretty young waitress approached our table, good thing too because I was about to call her out.

"Hi, my name is Tammie and I'll be your server today. First can I start you off with some drinks?" she asked us while staring hard into Ray's eyes.

She was a cute chick, a little skinny though. I was feeling her short hair cut. Her hair was curly in an asymmetric bob with light auburn highlights.

"For us," I motioned at Mocha and I, "lemonade light ice. And for him a Pepsi cold but no ice please." I knew them like the back of my hand and when she heard no complaints Tammie wrote it down on her little note pad.

"Ok, got it," Tammie said. "Are you guys ready to place your orders?" She smiled at Ray with eyes that said she hoped he wanted to place an order for her.

"Let me get two bacon cheeseburgers, and a crispy chicken Caesar salad if you don't mind," Ray smiled back at her.

"One of those burgers better be for me Ray, you know I ain't fucking with no salad!" Mocha exclaimed acting like her loud self again.

Our waitress laughed at Mocha's comment as she scribbled some more in her note pad.

"Ok, I'll get this right out," and with one more flirtatious look to Ray she went to put in our order.

"Damn is she switching hard enough?" Mocha shook her head. "Bitches go crazy over you Ray. I personally don't see it," she teased.

"Whatever," Ray waived her comment off. "These bitches just want somebody to save them, and I'm not that nigga. Especially after Shira's nasty ass."

"That dumb bitch," I got pissed off at the mention of her name.

Shira was Ray's ex who had faked a pregnancy with his baby. Long story short I called her out on it, she got mad, and I broke her jaw. My outer layer may have been prissy, but I came up in the streets. Growing up with my mom and her men seeing death and violence was nothing. I honestly had wanted to break more than just her jaw for trying to cash out on my cousin, but she dropped after one hit so what could I do? Don't fuck with my family; I guess she learned her lesson because her face was no longer seen in Detroit.

"Ray make sure your dick is strapped at all times, these hoes these days have no morals," I told him seriously.

"Chill Say!" Ray told me. "I'm not checking for a bitch right now. I'm all about my paper."

"That don't mean you aren't fucking them!" Women were nasty. Too quick to try and trap a nigga with money. I guess when it came down to it I was as over protective of him as he was over me.

Tammie came back with our drinks and confirmed that our orders should be out within a few minutes. I sipped my lemonade and the three of us sat in silence for a few moments waiting for our food to arrive. When it finally did we all dug in like we hadn't eaten in ages. I took a pause from eating and stared at Ray going to town on his burger. I knew the time was now or never.

"What?" Ray asked going to town on his burger.

I figured then was a better time than any to ask him the question that I'd been dying to ask. I was going to butter it up but I decided not to. Ray and I had always been straight forward with each other and I wasn't about to change that.

"When are you going to put me on?" I just came out and asked like it was nothing.

As soon as the question was out of my mouth the two of them stopped chewing their food abruptly. Mocha hadn't realized how serious I was until that very moment, and I didn't think she knew what to say. I hadn't warned her that I was going to bring the matter to Ray but the look on her face as she looked at Ray awaiting his answer let me know she was on my side. I knew Ray hadn't expected that question either, but he regained his ability to speak quickly and wiped the surprise from his face.

"Shut up with that shit Sadie, you don't know what you're asking for shorty," Ray said putting a fry in his mouth.

"Nah real shit Ray, you think I'm playing?" I lowered my voice although the restaurant was very noisy. "I've been thinking about this for a while now. You think I would bring this shit to you without thinking it through? I've done all my research on this shit. I lived the lifestyle for so long; I know what I'd be getting myself into. I just need you to say yes."

"That's funny," Ray scoffed. "I didn't know you could study to be a drug dealer. But since we're talking real shit Sadie they call this shit game, but ain't nobody playing with it. One way in and no way out, everybody's not made out for this life, especially not my little cousins. So quiet that noise."

"Get the fuck outta here with that shit Ray! You knew who my momma was and the shit she was about. I was raised around the shit, so I guess you can say I'm already in it. Blood deep! You fuckin' know this! I just need a connect and a starting point. And don't tell me what I'm cut out for because niggas probably said the same thing about you. But now look at you."

"You don't get it Say. From the outside lookin' in shit looks all gravy. You see my pockets full and my whip you would think it was easy. Nah. You have to be ready every second of the day to pull the trigger on a nigga. You have to come to terms with the fact that most niggas *ain't* loyal. It's more than them little niggas you see on the corners making those baby ass sales, this is a business. This is about the city, and to be all the way real. It's not too happy right now."

"Because of Coopa? So why you working for him then?" I inquired not quite getting where Ray was going with what he was saying.

"I already told you I don't work for that nigga. I work with him, and you wouldn't understand Sadie," Ray sighed.

"Enlighten me then Ray!" I raised my voice a little.

"Sadie, not right now," Mocha lightly touched my leg.

I sighed and backed down, but I was not finished. Ray was confusing me. He was saying he didn't work for Coopa, he worked with Coopa. But if Coopa was king of Detroit, what was the difference? I reluctantly continued eating my salad. I would have gotten up and walked out had it not been for the fact that I didn't drive my car.

"Say look," Ray started but was interrupted by the ringing of his phone. "Hello?" He answered.

"You ok?" Mocha asked me while Ray spoke into his phone.

"I'm fine," I lied.

"I just can't believe you were serious about this shit," Mocha said to me shaking her head.

Before I could reply I heard Ray's voice get louder.

"What the fuck do you mean nigga?" Ray was calm but his voice held an underlying anger. His whole demeanor had changed in a matter of seconds.

Mocha and I exchanged confused looks as we continued listening to Ray's heated conversation.

"I'm on my way. When I get there you better hope that shit reappears otherwise all ya'll muhfuckas is dead. Ask you to do one simple fuckin thing and you can't even do that. Coopa know?"

I heard the voice on the other end of the phone speaking quickly.

"Nah fuck that shit nigga, I keep you muhfuckas strapped. If Coopa's shit is gone then that means all of you should be dead. Period. I'm pulling up in five."

Ray hung up the phone and pulled out a hundred dollar bill from the pocket of his Levis.

"Let's go," He said dropping the bill on our table.

"Ray what's going on?" I asked trying to keep my pace with him in the coldness of the winter air. He ignorcd me and got in the truck. "Ray what the fuck is going on?" I asked again.

"You want this life?" Ray finally answered. "You want to be part of this fuckin' game? I'm about to show you what happens to niggas who fuck up in it."

♟ CHAPTER 3

Ray pulled up to a house about five blocks away from Grandma Rae's and the car was silent. The house wasn't much of a looker with the white paint chipping and the brick stairs leading to the front door crooked. In the driveway there was a brand new black Mercedes coup not even plated yet. It was a little dirty, since there were all types of dirt and snow on the ground. Ray parked behind it and got out of the car without a word to Mocha and me. I wasn't about to just sit in the car so I hopped out after him. By the time Mocha got out of the car Ray was already inside of the house.

"What the fuck is going on?" Mocha huffed in my ear as we made our way to the door.

I just shrugged, I didn't know what was about to happen. But when I looked at Ray's face while he was driving I knew something serious had gone down. We strolled through the door after Ray without knocking and as soon as we entered I felt as though I was entering a crime scene. The place was trashed. The living room was right when you walked through the door and all the furniture was flipped over. The television screen had a big hole in it and was lying on its side. There was a big tan couch flipped at such a crazy angle. I felt and heard the crunching of glass as Mocha and I made our way to the back of the one story house towards the kitchen. I knew whatever had happened hadn't been any good, and listening to Ray's voice travel from the kitchen I knew he wasn't happy. When Mocha and I entered the kitchen we saw four men other standing before Ray. Fear read all over their faces and anguish was all over Ray's. They were lined up in front of the refrigerator and when we made our entrance their eyes shifted to us. We stood away to the farther right side out of the way to observe the scene at hand. Ray ignored us and kept his eyes on the men before him.

"So what the fuck is up?" Ray put his hands in his pockets and shrugged his shoulders. "My man Jay here," he nodded his head at one of the light skinned men standing closer to Mocha and I, "said you got hit a few hours ago. Everything is gone, is that right?"

Nobody dared to speak. Ray had them spooked, and to be honest I was a little shook too. Ray's voice was low and calm, but deadly. His vibe controlled the temperature of the room, and the room was cold. He walked to one of them men to the far left end of the kitchen.

"What happened Little?" He asked him.

Little's name fit him perfectly. He was short and dark skinned with big fat French braids in his hair. He blinked rapidly with Ray less than a foot away from him and seemingly tried to think of his answer.

"Man Ray, those niggas just busted u-up in here. I don't know who the fuck been talking but they knew this was a trap," Little's high pitched voice stuttered.

"So you just let them take the shit?" Ray asked the questions, but it wasn't a question.

"N-Nah man. They was strapped h-heavy Ray—"

"Nigga each and every one of you muhfuckas have a burner!" Ray barked, the calm gone from his tone. "You muhfuckas weren't on you're A-game if you let some niggas walk up in this bitch and take the shit! Just cause they had guns huh? Nah something in this fucking story ain't adding up."

I inhaled sharply not knowing what was going to happen next. Ray went to stand in front of the tall guy standing next to Little. The man ran his hand over his fade haircut and had to force himself to look at Ray.

"You and Shy ain't do shit either, huh Tre?" Ray shook his head at the two caramel skinned men in the middle. Both were rocking the fade haircut.

None of the men looked younger than 20 or older than 25, but I would probably never know their ages. I heard Mocha's quick breaths beside me and I wanted to comfort her but didn't want to move.

"They would have killed us man!" Tre tried to reason.

"Then you should have died!" Ray barked again. "All four of y'all are pussies, you lack what we need in this business. Brains."

Ray then did something I wouldn't have expected at a time like that. He began laughing, hard. He waived a finger at the four of them and shook his head.

"Enough with the games though, I'm done entertaining the bullshit," he told them. "What's funny to me is that the only people who know about this house are Coopa, me, and you four. We are the only ones who also know when the product and money will even *be* in this bitch. So you know what I'm getting at right?" He nodded his head at them. "One or all of you niggas is a snake. And I don't need any snake ass muhfuckas on my team. Fifty stacks gone. Twenty bricks gone. I'ma just say this shit, you niggas are bold as hell."

"Nah man—" Jay tried to say.

"Shut the fuck up!" Ray got in his face causing him to jump back. "When I lose money it's not a good thing. But when Coopa loses money," Ray removed a 9 mm pistol from his waist, "niggas die."

My heart began beating uncontrollably fast. I couldn't believe what was happening, but then again I could.

"Oh shit," Mocha breathed grabbing my arm and trying to back us further into the kitchen wall.

"Now what the fuck really happened?" Ray asked screwing a silencer on his gun. "Jay that's a nice Mercedes out front. Looks like you just came up on some money, or are about to."

Ray and Jay locked eyes and there were a few seconds of silence. Out of the corner of my eye I saw Shy and Tre reach for their hips but before they could even aim I heard two small *spiffs*. Two round circles appeared in the middle of their foreheads and the refrigerator behind them was sprayed with blood. Beside me Mocha jumped but didn't make a sound.

"Ray you know I wouldn't set no shit like this up!" Little pleaded like a little bitch.

"I don't know," Ray cocked his gun. "That's why all of you have to die. Disloyal niggas...well they're just disloyal. And frankly I'd rather be safe than sorry."

He fired again and Little slumped. His eyes averted back to Jay who was literally shaking where he stood. I watched the scene before me like I was at an opening at midnight for the latest comedy.

"Jay, Coopa put you in charge nigga and this is what you do? I know those niggas weren't smart enough to come up with no shit like this. What the fuck man?"

"Ray," Jay threw his hands up. "Come on bro, we boys!"

Ray smirked at his futile attempt at throwing their friendship into play.

"Boys?" Ray spat. "Nigga we ain't boys.

"Man alright, coo. But you and I both know Coopa ain't doing shit for the city. That nigga don't give a fuck about nobody but his fuckin self. Not even the niggas out here in the streets everyday putting in work for *that* nigga. Fifty G's ain't shit to him! He's sitting on millions, fuck him! I have to eat son, got shit I have to handle. And since that nigga ain't giving why not take? Ray the streets are hungry and they're talking."

"Talking?" It seemed that some of the things Jay was saying sparked Ray's interest although his gun never lowered.

"Yea nigga. Talking. Muhfuckas don't like how Coopa been handling his business, even called his product bullshit. You know better than me Ray. You know Coopa ain't doing right in the game."

"Alright Jay," Ray nodded. "I feel you on what you're saying and all but who the fuck are you to take matters into your own hands? Robin Hood nigga?"

"Real shit Ray, everybody knows Coopa wouldn't be shit without you. That nigga would have been fell off if you weren't on his team. You should be running shit, not him. This money could be the start of ya empire nigga. And I would be on your team."

"First off nigga, I know all of this. Secondly I plan on being king pin sooner than later, but when it happens why the fuck would I want a snake like you on my team? You're a smart nigga though just not smart enough."

"Ray—"

"Did you think I was stupid when you called me with that bullshit ass story? As soon as I walked in this bitch I smelled the lie in the fuckin air. Oh and I saw that the board you dumb muhfuckas flipped the couch over was loose. This shit ain't nothing new to me, Sadie go pull that shit up."

"W-what?" I asked. I had forgotten that they could see Mocha and I.

"Go pull that board up," he instructed again never taking his cold eyes off of Jay.

I pried my arm away from Mocha and did as I was told. I walked back into the small living room area, glass crunching under my feet, towards where the upside down tan couch was. The one I saw once we entered the house. I used my body to scoot it to where I had access to the board underneath it and sure enough it was slightly lifted aloof from the other boards. I pulled it and it easily broke away from the floor. Underneath it was a long black duffle bag and a metal suitcase. I grabbed both, even though they were a little heavy and lugged them back into the kitchen. I dropped both in front of Ray and Jay but curiosity got the best of me. I knelt down and unzipped the duffle bag revealing at least twenty bricks of cocaine wrapped neatly. I also opened the suitcase and saw more Ben Franklin then I'd ever seen up close in person. I stood back up and looked at Ray who looked back at me and then back at Jay.

"Sadie what do I always tell you and Mocha?" he asked me .

I saw his right arm raise and I took a deep breath and whispered, "All your niggas ain't loyal."

I could still taste the words on my lips when one final shot rang out.

♟ CHAPTER 4

A few weeks passed since the incident at the trap house and Ray harbored some guilt for letting Mocha and Sadie see it go down. But because of what he was planning he knew they had to see it. He was planning something big, and he needed to break them into the business somehow. So his guilt was quickly succumbed by "fuck it." Deep down he did not want them to be part of the life that he lived every day, but to be honest besides his best friend Tyler they were the only other two people that he trusted with his life. Ray was born and raised in Detroit and he'd seen a lot of things; death, betrayal and hatred. He'd rarely seen love or "real." Real niggas were a thing of the past only to be replaced by clones of the real thing. Everybody knew that nothing was better than the original. Ray wasn't raised around riches or fame but once he got the money he became accustomed to it. He was a hood celebrity just as everyone major down with Coopa's operation.

Sadie and Mocha were well known as well, Tyler's younger sister Marie too. They were the princesses in the hood. Before they went to college, Mocha and Sadie went nowhere without at least five niggas with them. The two of them were so much alike, but so different. Sadie was well structured, he'd always known she didn't want to go to school, but he agreed with Grandma Rae when she said that's where she needed to be. Sadie had something he didn't see in a lot of niggas. She had a "Get That Shit" attitude and could back that shit up ten folds. Ray trusted her with everything he had and she had to be on his team. Just like he leveled Coopa's mind he knew Sadie would do that for him. She would keep him from making any drastic decision that could potentially ruin the uprising of his operation.

Mocha was efficient; she was the type of person who could tell if something was out of place with one glance. Ever since she'd come to stay with them he noticed how good with money she was. Counting it, flipping it, and doubling it. She was about it; Grandma Rae never had to give her a dime. He needed that on his team as well. Tyler was Ray's right hand man it. Tyler was the type of nigga who talked with his finger. Once you crossed him, you crossed him. He'd been laying niggas six feet under with the .45 since the age of eighteen. He didn't have a heart and if he did it only extended out to the four of them. Kill or Die Slow, that was the code that Tyler lived by. He had to fight his whole life and that right there made him the perfect general for The Last Kings.

The Last Kings…Ray had been repeating it in his head for the last few months of planning. He felt as if they were the last real niggas in the world and for that they should be treated as royalty. The last of a dying breed. He knew that from what the four of them witnessed growing up that they were strong enough to endure the hardships of a hustler. He knew right away that when brought to the table Sadie would be down. He saw the look in her eyes when she saw all that money. He also knew that as long as Sadie was down for the cause

Mocha would be too, they were ride or die. He was just waiting for their call. What Jay had said about Coopa losing touch with the streets was more right than anyone even knew, but he had kept that information to himself as he plotted his takeover. He knew Coopa would soon fall off, but before that happened Ray planned to be on his way to the top. Never had Ray been a sneaky person, but business was business. He wasn't going to rob Coopa of anything he had earned during his reign. He was just going to take Detroit by storm and in no time Ray was sure that the streets would be calling his name. Not Coopa's.

♟ CHAPTER 5

S ay are you alright?" My mind heard Mocha speaking to me but couldn't register her words. I was lost in my own thoughts trying and hoping they would fall into place.

The only thing that had been on my mind that whole time was the money. Surprisingly the fact that Ray killed four men before my eyes didn't bother me. I knew what my cousin did. It was just the life of a hustler. That was probably petty shit to him. Since he did it so effortlessly, with no fear. I admired that and I knew that I wanted that life. The power and money enticed me. Mocha hadn't said a word to me about it. It was like she was trying to put it in the back of her mind. Or maybe she was just waiting for me to bring it up, either way there was a strange air between us and I felt it.

"Bitch I know you hear me talking to you!" Mocha's voice was finally able to snap me out of my own head.

"Yea?" I rolled over on my bed to look at her. "What?"

"So you were just going to ignore me?" Mocha said sitting legs crossed on her bed.

"My bad," I said. "I was just thinking about some things. What did you say?"

"I asked your rude ass if you were ok. You've been acting different."

"Nah I'm good Mo. Just been thinking." I knew what she was going to ask next and I honestly didn't want to answer.

"About what?" She asked just like I knew she would.

I just shrugged my shoulders but I knew she wasn't going to let it go that easy.

"About what Sadie? Fuck! Why won't you talk to me?" She stood up in her sweats and came to sit on my bed beside me. I moved away from her a bit not wanting her to touch me.

"Mo chill. I've just had some things on my mind."

"Word? Like what?" Mocha pressed.

I knew she wasn't going to leave me alone until I told her the truth, so I did. I suddenly didn't care about what she thought. I took a deep breath and began speaking.

"I've decided that after this semester I'm dropping out of school. I might not even wait until then. College just isn't for some people and I'm in that 'some people' category. You know this shit, because I know you feel the same way. I could stay and waste even more of my fuckin' life, but for what though? To make Grandma Rae happy? What about my happiness? I want *money*. And I want it now. Like right now. I mean did you *see* that brief case of money Mocha? Ray toted that shit like it was chump change. I'm trying to get like that. I can hold my own against any nigga without an army behind me. I've been around this shit my whole life. It's only right that I take my rightful place in the game. Then take the throne; or one of them."

When I was done talking Mocha didn't say a word. Instead she stared into my eyes, and I looked back wondering how much of a dumbass she thought I was. When she finally did speak there was something different in her voice.

"Sadie it's a lot more that comes with that shit. Niggas get put on every day and never make it to Coopa's level. Instead they usually end up six feet under. You know, you watch the news just like I do. Niggas have to constantly watch their backs; muhfuckas are snakes especially if they see a bitch getting paid big bucks. So are you sure you want to take a blind dive into this shit?"

I didn't even have to think about it.

"Rats are going to rat and snakes are going to hiss. The game will never change Mocha and the potential danger doesn't scare me...it excites me. Shit makes me want to cum. I'm almost twenty years old and I know this is what I want to do."

"How are you going to do it? Huh? Are you going to be out on the corners selling that shit yourself? So you can get bumped up by the feds?"

I could tell Mocha was getting frustrated, but I also could tell that she knew like I knew that my mind was made up. I shrugged my shoulders at her again.

"Ray has my back," I answered her simply.

"Ray doesn't want you to live that lifestyle. Didn't you hear what he was saying?"

"No," I shook my head disagreeing with her. I thought about my cousin, I knew him better than anyone, even his best friend. "He wouldn't have let us see that shit if he was serious about me not being in the game." I saw a look of understanding spread across Mocha's face. "He was testing us Mocha. I don't know what the fuck Ray has planned. You heard what that dude said about Coopa and I could tell by Ray's face that it was true. I know my cousin; he's just waiting for me to call."

It took me a while to put two and two together, but I'd finally figured it out. Ray could have easily dropped Mocha and me off at our dorm before he went to handle his business but instead he took us with. He wanted to see how we reacted to the cut throat life he lived. He had always been like that, ever since I'd come to live with Grandma Rae. He was always testing me. But little did he know, I was ready. Mocha gave a long sigh and shook her head, some of her curls hung loosely from her ponytail.

"Ok Sadie, if this is what you want...I'm down bitch. But if I die I'm killing your ass."

♟ CHAPTER 6

While Mocha was in her English class I decided to pay my Grandma Rae a visit. I felt a little guilty especially since I was planning to go against her wishes with my schooling, but I couldn't help the fact that I missed her. I always liked to check on her just to see how she was getting along. I used the key she'd given me to enter her house and of course I instantly smelled a wonderful aroma coming from the kitchen.

"Grandma Rae?" I yelled out into the one story house closing the door quietly behind me.

I took my coat off and put it on a hanger in the hallway closet. To my right was Grandma Rae's living room. It was a nice size with black leather furniture sitting on the softest carpet. There was a black wooden table in front of the furniture and the entertainment center was against the wall. Her TV made the one at the dorm look like a baby. I kept straight going towards the kitchen where the smell was coming from and saw a shadow bustling around in the light.

"Grandma Rae?" I called out once more.

"In here chile!" she yelled back at me from the kitchen.

I entered the kitchen and saw my grandmother in a cute peach jogging suit outfit, an apron, and house slippers. Although she had silvery gray hair that fell just above her ears Grandma Rae didn't have a wrinkle on her body. She had the high cheekbones of a runway model and sharp brown eyes just like me and Ray.

"Mmm! Grandma Rae what you cooking?" I set my purse on the high six seating kitchen table and went over to where she was over the stove.

"Just some cornbread, macaroni and cheese, yams and chicken," she told me wiping her hands. "You hungry baby?"

"You know I am!" I said. My mouth was watering.

She made me a plate and I took it to the table to dig in. The first bite was pure perfection and I didn't know how I was surviving without her cooking at the dorm. I knew everybody said their grandma could cook, but my grandma cooked as well as Whitney Houston sang. There was no one better, well in Detroit. Her dream at one point in time was to open her own restaurant, but then she got pregnant and married a man who felt she would do better as a house wife. Whenever she spoke about her dreams and not being able to follow them; I always noticed the sadness in her eyes. I think that was why she wanted Mocha and me to go to school so bad, to make it and be something one day. I just wished I could live up to her expectations. I didn't have any dreams of a career. Well an honest career that is. Ever since I was young watching my mother's hustler boyfriends come and go, the money they all had. I began doing the research of drug cartels because I knew I wanted that life. I wanted to lead the biggest drug cartel Detroit had ever seen. I wanted it all, and if I were to tell my grandmother that was life I wanted to live I was almost certain it would break her heart.

"What's wrong with you girl?" Grandma Rae stood over me staring with a concerned expression. "You look like somebody stole your man or something'!"

"No I'm fine Grandma Rae," I laughed at her comment. "I was just focused on my food."

Grandma Rae gave me a skeptical look but she left me alone.

"Where's that girl Mocha at? I barely ever see the two of you apart! Like two peas in a pod you two are," she sat down at the table with me.

"She had class and I just was tired of being cooped in that dorm," I told her.

"Well make sure you take that girl a plate. You know she loves my cornbread," she waived her finger at me.

"Her ass does too," I said under my breath taking my last few bites of food.

"What?" Grandma Rae asked not hearing what I said.

"Oh nothing," I told her. "How have you been Grandma Rae? I see Ray is still keeping you fly."

"Yea you know that boy loves spending' his money on me," she shook her head and began cleaning the kitchen. "I keep telling' that boy to save his money! Buying' me all this designer shit, I'm sixty-five years old! What do I need Gookie for?"

"I think you mean Gucci grandma," I giggled at her horrible pronunciation of the word.

"That's exactly why I don't need it!"

"Whatever," I said still laughing.

"I just wish he would settle down. When I don't hear from him I can't help but to worry. I know what he does and I don't like it not one bit!"

I felt my head fall slightly; I couldn't look her in the face. I heard her sigh and continue sweeping.

"But he's grown now and has to find his own way. I know that money is addictive, but it's dangerous. Patty down the street just got a call last week saying her grandson was murdered. He was two years younger than Ray, I don't know what I would do if I got a call like that," she put her hand on her heart. "I thank God every day that you and Mocha are safe at the dorm getting your education. I just wish Ray would have stayed and got his! He's a smart boy, too smart to be running the streets!"

I didn't speak, I couldn't. I felt too guilty and that was a feeling I was trying to avoid. I knew my actions would hurt her and I didn't know if I was strong enough to handle that. Grandma Rae had always been there for me and gave me everything I needed. Now I was planning to basically betray her. I felt like a snake in the grass and I wanted to leave before I had to lie to her too.

"How's school coming' along honey?" Grandma Rae's voice was back to being soft and sweet.

Well so much for not wanting to lie.

"Umm, it's ok," I answered. Not completely a lie.

I'm just planning on dropping out to start the biggest drug cartel Detroit had ever fuckin seen, I confessed in my mind.

"That's good, make sure you and Mocha are keeping them grades up," she said.

"Yes ma'am," I grabbed my purse and stood to leave. "It was nice seeing you Grandma Rae, I'm about to get back before Mocha think I got kidnapped."

"Ok honey, take this plate to that girl!" she handed me a heavy plate covered in foil. "And it was nice seeing you too. Oh and if you see Ray can you give him this?" She handed me a few envelopes that had Ray's name on them. "He keeps forgetting to take them. Call me to let me know you got home safe hear? And baby?"

"What's up Grandma Rae?"

"You have a special heart," she started.

"And I'm going to do great things Grandma I know," I finished for her smiling. She said that whenever she saw me. I gave her small frame a hug and made my way to the front door. "Love you!" I called back to the kitchen before closing the door.

I walked quickly to my two door coupe in the cold with the plate warm in my hands .I got in my car and set the plate on the passenger seat and began to eye the mail. I had the strongest urge to rip both envelopes open just to see a part of Ray's life I wouldn't see any other time. Don't open it Sadie, I told myself. But after about one minute of a great debate in my head I found myself ripping the first envelope open. What was inside made my eyes bulge. It was a bank statement that said Ray had just shy of half a million dollars in his account. I wasted no time in opening the second envelope. Inside that one was also a bank statement, that one with only two hundred thousand. Just as I was about to pull off en route to Uncle Rojer's auto shop my phone began vibrating in my back pocket.

"Hello?" I said knowing it was Mocha calling without looking at the caller ID.

"Where are you at?" Mocha asked. "You never go anywhere without telling me."

"Damn mom, I didn't think you would be that worried," I said pulling off away from the curb in front of Grandma Rae's house.

"Shut up bitch, after the shit you were talking I thought you had gone out and done something stupid," Mocha sounded as if she was seriously worried about me so I couldn't even be agitated.

"No, not yet anyways. I haven't talked to Ray yet. As a matter of fact what are you doing right now?" I asked Mocha.

"The dorm obviously bitch, how else would I know you aren't here?" I could hear her eyes rolling.

"Well get in your car and meet me at Uncle Rojer's shop. You know Ray always helps out on Thursdays, I would rather talk to him about this shit face to face."

"Ok," Mocha told me. "I'm leaving now."

"I'll see you there," I was about to hand up the phone.

"Say?" Mocha asked.

"What?"

"What if he says no? Then what?" She asked in all seriousness.

"Then nothing," I told her. "He's not going to say no."

"Well look what the cat done dragged in!" Uncle Rover greeted both Mocha and I when we walked into the garage. He and Ray were in the middle of working on a raggedy looking green pickup truck when they heard our footsteps.

Ray turned around and smiled when he saw us.

"I was wondering when you two were going to come looking for me," he said wiping his hands off on a rag hanging from the pockets of his dirty overalls. "About a day late though."

For some reason seeing Ray was different to me for me. For once I didn't look at him as my big cousin who protected me and kept my pockets filled. I saw him as the street saw him, his presence demanded respect. He was the epitome of a boss and I knew then that soon Coopa's mistakes in the streets would soon get him caught up. I was at a loss for words with my cousin for a moment, but quickly I regained my composure. He might've thought I was shook; but really I was in awe.

"How are you doing Unc?" I asked my uncle not knowing what to say to Ray.

Uncle Rojer was a forty-four year old heavier set man, which was odd due to the fact that he was almost as tall as Ray.

"Tired!" Uncle Rojer's loud voice boomed. "Seems every motherfucka in this city done broke their car!"

"It's what's bringing in your money though Unc," Ray chuckled.

"Yea, yea," Uncle Rojer began walking to the door leading to the inside of his shop. "Just make sure you lock up the shop."

Uncle Rojer waived "bye" to us and when I heard an engine start and car drive off I knew he was gone. I went and sat on a chair next to the truck that was previously being worked on.

"I have to go to the ladies room," Mocha excused herself from the garage and I knew what she was doing. "I'll be right back." She shot me a look as she exited to the inside of the shop and I knew she would be gone until things with Ray got squared away.

"So much for being ride or die," I said. I was hoping I would have her support in the matter of the conversation with Ray

"So what's up shorty?" Ray threw his towel to the side and pulled up a chair directly in front of me.

He knew what I wanted. He was testing me again. I wasn't going to let him intimidate me, especially with what I was asking for. What I wanted wasn't just given, it came at a cost. I had to prove that I was worth it.

"You know what's up Ray. You've known since that day at the restaurant," I wasn't going to lie. The way he was looking at me with those sharp eyes again I was almost unsure of myself. "Regardless if you help me or not you know what lifestyle I want to live. The lifestyle I'm going to live. I'm not like my mom. You know the shit I dealt with coming up in Grandma Rae's house. Everybody knew about my momma being a hoe and was sure I would be just like that."

Ray's eyes stared intensely into mine; he was on top of every word escaping my mouth. He knew all of the stories about my mother. Shit he probably knew some that even I didn't know, so I knew he understood what I was saying. But I needed him to *feel* what I was saying. I was only nineteen but in my mind I was double that, I needed him to see that as well.

"In some ways I'm just like her, we're obviously attracted to the same things. But the difference is that I plan to be on top, never on the bottom. So what's up boss?"

I looked at Ray to see his exact reaction and but all I got was a look of sadness.

"Don't look at me like that," I said sternly to him. "Don't you fucking dare look at me like that!"

Ray sighed before finally nodding his head.

"Ok...ok it seems to me whether or not I help you you're determined to make it into the game somehow. I would rather you be with me than against me, I know your drive. But just give me a minute aight?" Ray asked me.

"How long Ray? When Coopa has your ass laid out in a ditch?" I asked him becoming upset that he was really trying to give me the run around. "Real shit Ray the time is now or never."

I didn't like the fact that Ray was basically Coopa's flunky especially when Ray was the brains behind every operation. He was the reason Coopa's pockets stayed filled and I didn't understand why Ray stood for it. Ray never had it in him to follow; he always had to be in the lead. But Coopa had a team and a connect while Ray had only himself. So it seemed. If he was going to start it was going to have to be from scratch and I was willing to help build with him. Instead of responding to my words Ray stood up and grabbed a duffle bag.

"I have to go get dressed. I'ma fuck with y'all later ok?" He said and with that left the garage.

I sat there dumbfounded staring at the green truck. I couldn't believe he had just cut me off like that, like my conversation wasn't worth his time. I heard the door open to the shop open once more and I looked up to see Ray standing there staring at me.

"Keep your phone on ok shorty?" He said smiling. "Something big is about to go down."

Before I could inquire on what the hell he was talking about Ray was gone again. Seconds after his exit Mocha reappeared. She saw the bewildered look on my face and held up her hands.

"What just happened?" she asked me wanting to know all of the details.

"I-I don't know," I said honestly. "Come on lets go."

I stood up to leave the garage and ponder over Ray's words.

"Did you get your answer?" Mocha pressed again walking after me.

"We'll see," I said and got into my car.

"I drove all the way down here for a fuckin' we'll see?"

"Yea," I told her. "You did. I'll see you back at home."

I started my car and sped off leaving her on the sidewalk to watch my exhaust. I knew that was rude since I'd told her to come meet me but whatever. I had too many of my own thoughts to sort through. If Ray didn't accept my "business" proposition I honestly didn't know what I was going to do with my life. I would rather be a broke homeless muhfucka on the street than stuck in a career I hated for the rest of my life. The streets were all I knew and there was money in them. So why not invest? I wondered what Ray was going to say when he called me, hopefully something good. Hopefully.

♟ CHAPTER 7

R ay handed the shiny silver keys back to the owner of the green pickup and closed up the shop once it drove off. Ray was no longer in the dirty overalls that he wore on the days he chose to work at his uncle's shop. He'd gone to the bathroom in his uncle's office and took a shower. When he emerged he looked like a new man, gone were the somewhat thuggish clothes he'd become accustomed to wearing. Replacing them was a light green Gucci button up that was slightly tucked into his tan Gucci slacks and on his feet he wore light green Gucci dress shoes to match. The shoes added a nice touch and with his dreads pulled back into a ponytail Ray's appearance was very suave. As soon as Ray put on his coat and stepped out of the shop to lock the door, an all black Mercedes with windows tinted so dark. You couldn't see who the passengers inside were slowed to a stop in front of the shop. Ray glanced down at the Rolex on his wrist gleaming back up at him. It read six o-clock.

Right on time, Ray thought to himself as he approached the vehicle.

Ray was supposed to be handling some business for Coopa. Word had it that another one of his houses had gotten hit. But if all went well that wouldn't be Ray's problem any longer, so he didn't answer his call. Lately Coopa had been on some funny shit with Ray but

Ray knew what was going on. He didn't speak on it, especially when people brought it to his attention that Coopa was losing his grip on the game. Ray knew he'd been doing the thing that lead to every great hustler's demise. He'd started smoking his own product. Ray had always been observant and he could tell by the slight twitch in Coopa's right eye and by the way he rubbed his hands together that he was on drugs. Those were two things he didn't do before, and as soon as he started doing those two things his empire began to fall. Coopa had started making poor choices in business and putting snake ass niggas on. Coopa was putting his trust in all the wrong people. Within a year almost half a million dollars came up unspoken for. No one knew this but Ray and Coopa, and that was another reason Ray didn't trust him. Coopa noticed all of that from the beginning but hadn't done anything to prevent it except dead the niggas he actually found out were stealing from him. Why would he make an effort to save a man who couldn't save himself? The game was going to have its way with Coopa, Ray wasn't a fortune teller but he could see that. Ray knew when he first started working with Coopa no good would come from it. His pockets would stay fat for a while. He knew eventually would the time would come when he would take over. Ray had the mindset of a boss and a swagger of a hustler. He was intelligent, ruthless, and got every job done without a blemish. He knew that in order to set the shit off right. He would need a connect with some kill. It was backwards a little bit because Ray had helped Coopa add on to his empire only to take it into his own grasp. He knew Coopa wasn't going to bow without a fight. Ray had heavy artillery but Coopa had heavy artillery and several niggas who were too scared of him not to ride. Ray felt like an ant in the shadow of a shoe until one night an unavailable number hit his phone.

The voice on the phone was someone Ray had never heard before, but he knew it belonged to someone of Italian heritage. They informed him that they'd been watching him very closely and they liked the shit he did. How he handled his business. Told him that they couldn't say much over the phone but to be ready at six o'clock PM the following Thursday in business attire. "None of that thug shit." Any other time Ray would have been suspicious of a set up, but something in him told him it wasn't.

Ray walked to the car and the door opened for him. Ray entered a car with three Italian habitants all dressed in black Armani suits. Ray wasn't gay by any means but he had a keen eye for fashion. Being fly at all times was a code to live by. Ray studied all of their hardened faces trying to read them and in turn they did the same to him. To Ray's surprised he recognized one of the men in the car as a man who'd been to his uncle's shop a few times for minor car problems. He'd told Uncle Rojer that he was just in town for a few days and wanted his vehicle inspected. His name was Vinny.

Vinny stared at Ray and was very impressed with his attire. He knew from the first day he met Ray that he was dealing with a potential boss, the way he knew numbers was impeccable. There was no getting over on him. He could see by Ray's poise that he was different. Unlike the two bit street hustlers he'd grown accustomed to seeing in Detroit. The majority of them weren't about business just quick cash, but with the information he'd dug up about Ray he knew he would be the perfect attribute to his cartel. Vinny needed to expand his work. He didn't want to control any territory. Just get off his product. He was looking to be the supplier, however, he needed someone trustworthy and business savvy enough to supply to. He'd heard about a cat named Coopa, but after scoping him out for a few days he saw how sloppy he handled his work. Too messy, he needed someone he could depend on. Not someone who would end him up in federal prison. After testing Coopa's product Vinny knew for a fact that the hunger in Detroit was real. Whoever Coopa was down with was definitely getting over. Nobody was fucking with a man who couldn't even deliver. Vinny heard about Ray through the grapevine and was pleased with what he scoped. He had one of his men contact him and ready a meeting as soon as possible. The streets of Detroit were getting hungry and Vinny had what their appetite needed.

"Gentlemen," Ray broke the silence nodding his head at the occupants of the Mercedes and they returned the gesture.

"I believe we met indirectly before," Vinny said holding his hand out from the far side of the backseat where he and Ray sat. "I am Vinny, and that's Eduardo," he nodded to the heavy set slick haired driver. "And that man right there is Stanley."

Stanley nodded at them from the passenger seat. His sleek black hair was combed up into a Mohawk making his beak like nose even more distinguishable. Stanley gave Ray the eye and Ray stared back wondering why the muhfucka was staring at him. Stanley then nodded his approval to Vinny who smiled wide. Vinny was a middle aged man. He'd come from a wealthy family of mobsters so he knew no other life than the grimy one he lived. He was very handsome and was known to be something like a womanizer, but only because money was the only bitch he loved.

"This my friends," Vinny pointed at Ray, "is the future! Ray you're not new to this, so let us get straight into business."

"I couldn't have said the shit better myself," Ray said cockily and got comfortable in his heated leather seat waiting for Vinny to continue.

"As I'm sure you know Coopa has some very unhappy customers. He doesn't have what the streets are looking for and pretty soon he's going to pay for it. Probably with his life or his dick; one of the two," Vinny's accent was laying on thick with every word spoken. "The city needs some new work...and a new king otherwise it's looking pretty dry."

"So what are you proposing Vinny?" Ray asked cutting to the chase. "You got some work for me?"

Vinny chuckled at Ray's boldness, but little did he know Ray was just as deadly as him.

"You know how this shit works, to rule you need a connect. I got what you're looking for," he told Ray staring seriously into his eyes. "I'm not going to lie. I've been watching your every move for a few days now and I like you kid. You're smooth, the little operation you have going on is nice. I just don't know yet if I can trust you."

Ray nodded, agreeing with what he said. He didn't trust their Italian asses either. He'd heard crazy things about the Italian cartel. They were up there with the Dominicans, definitely not anyone to fuck with on a beef level.

"But I know you're the man who can get the job done, what I'm saying Ray is I need you," Vinny said. "None of that homo shit, this is strictly business. I need my work in Detroit and I need you to push it."

Ray sat taking everything Vinny was saying in not trying to look too eager. But inside he couldn't believe his luck.

Damn these muhfuckas been following me? Ray thought to himself making a mental note to double security.

"You want me to just be down with this shit?" Ray asked. "I don't know you muhfuckas from a can of paint, so tell me what's really good?"

"I understand your caution Ray, we randomly contacted you and now we're offering you the place of a king. I can see where thoughts get skeptical, but I wouldn't even waste my time sitting here talking to you if this wasn't a serious business proposition. I need a yes or no answer in 30 seconds or I will take you back to your uncle's shop and we can pretend this conversation never happened...well until I send the choppers for you."

Damn these muhfuckas definitely aren't playing around, Ray thought. To be real they had me with that king shit.

"Aight, how much are we talking and when are we doing this shit?" Ray asked

"Smart man!" Vinny smiled pleased with Ray's answer.

Eduardo and Stanley smirked at each other from the front seat and Ray saw it, but he kept his cool. He knew he was playing ball in their field.

"I'm going to give you a little product first, just to see how fast you can get it off, and when you do I'll give you more," Vinny explained.

Ray listened but wasn't with that plan at all. He already had a plan formulated and he knew exactly what he was doing. Vinny was now just giving him a reason to go through with it instead of waiting.

"No fuck that," he said shaking his head surprising all of the passengers inside the vehicle. "If we're going to do this we're doing it my way. My city, my rules. I'm a grown ass man, ain't no fucking way I'm about to just let you *give* me any product. Off tops I'ma buy that shit and flip it in no time. Then I'll just re-up from there. I can't make a profit off another man's empire, been there done that. All I need from you is a team and artillery, I already have three ready to get this shit. I know once Coopa catches wind on what the fuck is going on it's going to be bloodshed. But honestly right now this money is more important," Ray told Vinny.

Vinny sat taken aback but was beyond impressed on how the business meeting was being flipped around on him. Ray was definitely the right pick for the job.

"What are you saying Ray?" Vinny asked him.

"What I'm saying is you need me as much as I need you. Otherwise, you would have never contacted me in the first place. Instead of putting yourself in some shit by fronting me any product I'll just buy that shit and start my own operation. I'm not stupid or new to this shit, but you do need new blood and that's me. I live and breathe the hustle and I'll dead a muhfucka quick over my paper," Ray told him. "I'ma need to test your product first to see if it's even worth the hassle."

"Of course," Vinny nodded. "Stanley?"

On cue Stanley handed Vinny a kilo of cocaine and a small pocket knife.

"Here you go," Vinny handed Ray the brick and sat back and watched already knowing the value of his own product.

Ray made a small incision in the brick and tasted a small amount. Ray had been in the business long enough to use that as a method to level grades of cocaine, and Vinny's product had passed the test. He nodded his head in approval. He already saw the dollar signs flashing before his eyes knowing he had the key to the city in his hands at that very moment.

"Alright coo, this is what I'ma have?" He had to make sure.

"Yes," Vinny informed him. "How many?"

"I'ma need 30."

"Five hundred thousand," Vinny said instantly and watched to see if Ray would back down due to the price.

"Done," Ray didn't even flinch. "I'll give you a drop off spot and we'll make the exchange."

Vinny smiled one last time knowing then that he'd made a long time business partner. He reached out and shook Ray's hand again.

"Alright, I'm going to set you up with this shit personally," Vinny said.

He liked how Ray conducted business. He was going to make his money regardless and now he had a permanent buyer, Vinny was very pleased. He didn't know the meeting would go like that, but truth be told he expected nothing less. They made plans to meet at a lowkey spot Ray knew the next day.

"The shit here is garbage. People pay good money for the shit they smoke, inject, or snort. Why not give them their money's worth?" Vinny said to Ray as they pulled back in front of Uncle Roger's shop. "Starting today Ray you are a king, not a street hustler. You're better than Coopa. Starting today Detroit is yours. I have two people perfect for this ...don't worry we did background check on these motherfuckers so loyalty is not a worry. You sure you can trust your people?"

"I'm one hundred percent sure," Ray told him getting out of the car.

"Alright...I'll see you soon kid," Vinny said and with that he pulled off.

Ray pulled his cell phone out watching the black Mercedes round the corner and leave his sights. He was about to tell Sadie, Mocha, and Tyler that he had a business proposition for them. After phoning them informing to meet him at his home Ray decided to take a walk through his hood. He changed from suit and tie to a casual Diamond muscle shirt and a pair of cargo shorts. His bullet proof vest snug on his torso ensured that no bullet would penetrate and the .45 on his hip dared a nigga to put his vest to use. He left his Escalade parked in the parking lot of the car shop and made his way on foot towards his Grandma Rae's house.

Putting his Wolf Grey 5's to use he worked his way through the neighborhood he grew up in. Everything in it was a familiar sight. The houses were run down, some yards cut and some weren't. Kids were running around like they didn't have any sense. Ray saw the swift moves of his little niggas hitting the block. Fiends were everywhere begging for shit but Ray didn't feed their hunger. None of the product they snorted could be tied back to him in anyway, they were too messy. The people his niggas served to were high rollers who had an addiction to the candy Ray provided. The feds had moved in and out of his block, even sent a couple of undercover cops to scope Ray's small operation. But when their bodies were found dismembered that never happened again. Ray didn't move any product on his block so any warrant to search it was deemed pointless. Out of all of the niggas Coopa put on Ray's operation was the cleanest. Ray had a list of clients he served and they bought in bulks not by the hit. They knew where a nigga would be posted on the block to place their order. A place and time would then be designated for a drop off and pick up. First of course the money would have to be wired into an account that was opened and closed that same day. Ray had work moving all through Detroit and he not only fed his block but everyone else's too. He kept the block cleansed of Coopa's work. It was smart but it was more out of respect for Grandma Rae.

Niggas all around the way showed him love as he passed them. The daylight completely gone only to be replaced by street lights Ray saw the streets come alive. It was rare to see Ray walking anywhere so many of the neighborhood rats tried to get his attention by switching quickly in front of him or saying "Hi," flirtatiously. Ray only gave head nods and kept it moving while he tried to gather his thoughts. As he walked and ignored the basic hoes cooing his name. He came across two of the most niggas he had pushing for him. D and Amann were posted on a street corner engaged in a conversation with two young women. They were bad and both had fat asses but when Ray was spotted the two women were immediately dismissed. D and Amann were both in 501 Levis and retro J's. Diamonds were glistening from their jewelry like the hood celebrities they were and they both gave Ray a respectful smile.

"My mans!" D shook Ray's hand. "The fuck you doing' out here walking' fam? We got Beamers and shit for all'at!"

Ray grinned because he was right. Bosses didn't walk, but in that instant he needed the air to clear his mind and a walk was what he needed.

"I'm chilling' fam," was Ray's simple response.

D and Amann were brothers. Not by blood but it couldn't make them any closer. Through thick and thin they had each other's back and their loyalty in each other was what embedded Ray's trust in them. Out of every nigga Ray had working the two of them put in the most work and brought home the most paper. They could hustle in their sleep, but the way they moved they never slept. At the age of twenty two they were also well tenured.

"What's been good though?" Ray asked stopping to talk for a minute.

"Shit, shit," Amann answered. "Working."

"Yea, niggas been putting in overtime it seems like just to fuckin' eat," D rubbed his hands together. "Upping prices."

"I see," Ray nodded already knowing.

He knew all that was going on, especially after the dumb niggas tried to hit Coopa's trap. Coopa was fuckin' up and Ray had to pick up his slack. He wasn't with that shit in the least bit. Unsatisfied clients made for angry workers. Everybody was just trying to eat and that was something Ray understood. Coopa wasn't as in tune with the streets as he once was when he was living in them. He was selfish and as long as his table was filled he didn't give a fuck about anybody else's. Ray respected him because it was his work that had indeed put him on but he also knew that once you lost touch with the streets there was no coming back from that.

"Aye let me rap to you two about some shit real quick," Ray said making a decision then to put them on with his operations. D and Amann knew automatically knew by his tone that they needed to listen to what was about to be said. "You two niggas put in work. Loyalty is something that's hard to come by in this day and age. When you got it you don't just throw the shit away. So I'd like to personally welcome you to The Last Kings. It's time to go to work."

♟ CHAPTER 8

W hen Ray came to me and Mocha about his business proposition; he called us to his home that was ducked off in the suburbs of Detroit. He set us down in his living room. Soon Tyler joined us as well. He then asked me how serious I was about taking my first step into the game. He told us that he'd just come across a business opportunity that he couldn't pass. He didn't give us the name of his connect, he just told us that he had some major work. Tyler was already down with the plan, and I was too. Mocha was the one who sat unsure. It made me a little agitated just because the idea of a drug cartel was her idea. The fact that she was trying to pussy out didn't sit right with me. What he was asking was dangerous I knew, but it wasn't like I would be new to the shit. I knew how to hustle, how to break it down, and how to make my money quadruple. My life had been pledged to the game at an early age. This would just be carrying out my destiny.

"You can't make muhfuckas respect you," Ray told Mocha and he pulled out two black boxes from underneath his long coffee table. "That's why you make them fear you. As long as you make your money and watch your back it doesn't matter what anyone thinks of you."

He slid the boxes across the wooden table towards Mocha and I. Lifting the top of mine my breath was short and sweet when I saw the inhabitants. Inside the box was a shiny 48 caliber pistol and two rounds next to it. I hesitated but I picked it up and held it firmly in my hand. It felt natural.

"R-Ray, I don't know," Mocha said staring at her hand gun. "This is crazy."

"Yea Ray," I had to agree with her. "Coopa is going to flip when he finds out about this shit."

Ray shook his head letting me know I was wrong.

"The difference between Coopa and me is that I'm not going to have you two on any corner making drops, that's sloppy and out of date. This is going to be a business; I don't have time to be hot in these streets with the feds on my ass."

"What happened to loyalty Ray?" Mocha asked him.

"Fuck that Mocha," Tyler countered. "I've been telling' my boy to strike out on his own for years now. Coopa don't know the first thing about being loyal shorty."

"Right," I agreed with Tyler. "Ray if you got us you know I'm down to ride for whatever," I felt the thug in me come out as I eyed my pistol and then Ray.

"Say I knew you would be down to ride," Ray smiled at me fondly. "What do you say Mocha? How about we make this a family affair?"

"You say that shit like you're asking me to join a club or something! This shit is serious; we're talking about a drug cartel! As in a drug ring...as in some Ashley Annette shit!"

"Antoinette," I corrected.

"Yes her! Fuck this is crazy Say...crazy!" Mocha stared at her pistol.

"Mocha, what do you want to be in life?" I asked catching her off guard by the question.

"What? I don't know, somebody who makes a lot of money. Shit I don't know!"

"A boss?" Ray referenced.

"A boss," I concurred.

Mocha sighed and eyed all three of us before she finally nodded her head submissively.

"Yes, a boss."

"Ok," I grabbed her hand. "Let's get this shit then; for the love of money right?"

Our eyes met for a moment seeming to connect us, making us one. Holding silent conversations was something we did when we were younger when she first came to stay with us. The words I spoke to her with my eyes were sincere. Finally Mocha blinked breaking eye contact and I knew she was in.

"Ok, I don't even give a fuck!" She rolled her eyes. "I'm just worried about getting trigger happy with this muhfucka!" Mocha aimed her pistol at Ray's white living room wall and mouthed "Pow."

I laughed happy we had our team formed.

"Coo," Ray nodded his approval eyeing everyone in the room. "We're a team now, so the only thing left to do is to make shit happen."

We did just that. Ray and Tyler already knew the rules of the game and I was a little tenured in it as well. Ray took us under his wing and in a matter of weeks Mocha and I knew everything about the dope game a man could teach us.

"Everything else just comes with the territory," Ray told us.

Ray had some change saved up from when he was working with Coopa because he went all out and bought a slew of laundromats, an apartment complex, an Italian restaurant, a hair salon and a strip club. Ray's work started spreading quickly like the flu bug through Detroit. No one knew who the carrier was, but everyone seemed to be feeling it. The team Ray set us up with was the truth. Besides Ray, Mocha, Tyler and I. There were four other additions to our fam. They were obedient and ready to ride out whenever or wherever. When it came to distributing and collecting they always delivered. I'd become fond of a little Latina chick named Adrianna, she was a feisty little thing. She always pulled in double her weight and being in the big leagues didn't scare her. She was older than me by a few years but she knew that I was the boss. She always made sure the money was counted right before it was delivered to Ray or myself. I fucked with her the long way.

It was my idea to start a VIP club for our top whole sale clients. They were the only ones eligible to be members after a thorough background check. Ray thought the idea was brilliant and decided to add a pleasure kick to it. The buyers could test our product while getting their dicks wet. The spot was underground literally. It was located in the basement of the Italian restaurant Ray had purchased. Tyler came through big time with his connect with the feds. Tyler broke him off a little paper here and there to be informed on the moves of the police. That way we always had some type of heads up. After that it was a wrap. It was clear that we were slowly but surely taking over the city. Ray had stopped fucking with Coopa completely and I knew that wasn't going to end well, but I trusted his judgment. Coopa wasn't the only one anymore with a team of riders. The city was slowly but surely climbing on Ray's back because he *gave* back. He wasn't the only one profiting from the weight of his wallet exceeding capacity. If anything popped off there would definitely be a war scene in the streets of Detroit. Ray made sure that Mocha and I were never alone wherever we went and told us to always stay strapped.

"Niggas hate seeing a come up," he always told us and I knew he was referring to Coopa.

After Mocha and I dropped out of school we began living with Ray in his home since it was big enough. Five rooms, four bedrooms, two kitchens, a theatre in the basement and this nigga even had the audacity to have a fucking fountain in his entry way. Those were just some of the highlights, Ray had really outdone himself with his house and I was proud that he'd come that far. One night when just me and him were home; I brought it to his attention while we counted stacks of money to maybe let Coopa in on the action, keep the love in the city. I didn't see the point in going to war in your own home town. The money would be doubled and be kept flowing, it made sense to me. However Ray disagreed.

"Nah Say, Coopa ain't the type to just shake hands and step down from the throne. Detroit is his in his eyes. Unless somebody knocks him down from his seat he ain't going' nowhere," he put me on game.

"So what are we going to do when he jumps?" I asked him. "'Cause you know that nigga is going to jump."

"You know what's going to happen Say," Ray touched the steel he kept on his waste. "That nigga is either going to bow down or lay down. My city ain't going down 'because a boss can't stay a boss, fuck that. It's all about this here."

He grabbed a stack of hundreds and waived them in the air.

"A nigga will do crazy things for this Sadie…just remember not to be that crazy," Ray told me and sighed. "Coopa is going to try and stop this shit, I'm on the rise and his position as kingpin is being threatened. But I know him he's not going to come for me directly, I know his style. He's going to come for what I hold dearest to my heart. You and Grandma Rae."

What Ray was telling me made sense. I then understood the reason why he made Mocha and I strolled the city with five goons each.

"I got niggas at her house around the clock," Ray informed me seeing the worry on my face.

"She's ok with that?" I asked astounded knowing Grandma Rae hated random muhfuckas in her home.

Ray grinned at me through the freshly twisted dread locks dangling freely in front of his face.

"Hell Nah Say, you know she would flip if she knew them niggas were there!"

I grinned too but then became serious again.

"Ray, I just want you to know I can handle myself," I told my cousin. It was rare when I got him to myself now-a days and I wanted to reassure him that letting me into his cartel wasn't a bad idea. "This shit is nothing to me. I'm not scared of a fuckin' Coopa or what he could potentially do to me. If you got me, I got you remember?"

Ray smiled and nodded his head.

"I feel you Say, and I know you can handle yourself. I'ma just make it so you never have to," Ray stood up and started dumping the money in bags preparing to make a drop to re up. "Where's Mocha?"

I shrugged my shoulders.

"She made a trip to visit a friend in Atlanta, she'll be back in a few days," I told him not letting it show on my face that I missed my best friend. I knew Mocha was from Atlanta, so I didn't mind her taking a few trips to her hometown.

It was rare when we weren't together, especially since we both dropped out of school to tend to business. I knew I wasn't going to be anybody's executive but the dopeman's so I didn't want to waste any more of my time. Ray was upset with the decision but we stood firm by it.

"You been coo?" Ray studied me where he stood.

"Yea, I've just been kicking it hard with Adrianna. That's my bitch, she's a fucking thug dude," I said thinking fondly of my new friend.

"Yea she's ride or die, I had to have her in on this shit. Loyalty is all I need. When Mocha gets back we're having' a meeting, there is some other shit I need to bring to the table. It's been a few months now and the money is rolling in, I need to know where y'all heads at?"

"Alright, I'ma hit that bitch up and tell her to get her ass home ASAP," I told him and pulled out my cell phone.

♟ CHAPTER 9

Ray wasted no time in holding his meeting once Mocha touched back down in Detroit. He had us meet in the dining room of our home and we sat around a table that sat ten. All but two of the chairs were filled and everybody who was supposed to be there was there. It was a still night in Detroit, the weather had finally begun to warm as we said goodbye to the winter season. The moon shone in on us all through the glass patio door beside the table glistening on the glasses of champagne presented before each of us. Tyler sat on Ray's right side while I sat on the left. Mocha sat beside me and Adrianna beside her. Devynn was a young beautiful dark skinned woman with long soft natural curls sitting atop of her head. She packed two heaters one on each thigh and fucking with her would give two clips a home inside your skull. In her case looks were very deceiving. She looked sweet but she had the bite of a tiger. I honestly thought I would have a problem with her but she was cool. I think she was scared of me, if only she knew I hadn't even taken my first life...directly anyways. Next to her sat D short for Deion. He was a big swole nigga. He didn't need his burner to rock a nigga to sleep, his fists were weapons themselves. His Jamaican heritage gave him a very distinct look, but not in a good way. D was, in other words, ugly as fuck. His dreads were short and thick and his eyes were too close together, but he knew how to hustle and aim a gun so he was good for our team. He also worshipped the ground Ray walked on; his loyalty was very much respected. He was good people. Last but not least was Amann. He had a smooth baby face but harbored a ruthless mentality. Since his girlfriend and two year old daughter were killed in the cross fire of a run in he thought with the 9 mm pistol that he had strapped to his waste. He'd lost everything so spilling blood was like spilling water to him. Amann was someone you sent in to get the job done. His heart was buried with the body of his baby. The only things he believed in were loyalty and getting money and anybody who got between that would surely get put to rest. I was in a room full of cold blooded kill-ers. People who put bullets in people like shots from the doctor, and I had never felt more at home.

Ray stood up from where he sat at the head of the table and eyed each and every person around him, even Tyler.

"Hello ladies and gentlemen," he started with a smirk. "If you're wondering why you're here then you need to get up and out of my fuckin' house."

No one moved, everyone knew what was up and Ray nodded his head.

"That must mean you know why you're here. You know who you are," Ray started to walk slowly around the rectangle table. We all glanced around becoming familiar with each other's faces.

We all knew of each other, but it was the first time we'd all been together in one room. We all had been making our solo shit trying to get the operation off the ground and get off the product Ray purchased from his mysterious connect in time to re up. I nodded my head at everyone around the table as my way of showing them that they were my new family now.

"This," Ray raised his hands motioning to everyone at the table, "is Team Mula, and that's exactly what the fuck we do. We get this dirty money quick and flip it even faster. I would also like to say congratulations. You've proved to me that you all are about this paper and it was you who built the foundation of this operation. I'm impressed...I've never seen a team of only eight people flip coke so fast. The profit I made off those bricks was more than even I expected. This is the start of a new movement; we're taking over this shit. It's time to show Detroit who the new heads of the city are!"

We all nodded our heads feeling empowered by Ray's words.

"I grew up in these streets watching the common street hustler slang dope on the corners. Watching their pockets fill quickly, their come up. Because of their flashiness and cockiness; I saw their demise too. That's not going to be us...kings live forever! We are the last fucking kings! *This*?" Ray pointed his two pointer fingers towards the ground. "This is the whole operation, here in this room. If I eat we all eat because kings never get hungry!"

The room remained silent and I appreciated the respect they all had for Ray. He stood over us as a leader...the head of Team Mula. He was a boss on a major come up and I would be lying if I said I didn't see him as the next king pin of Detroit. It was his time, and I think everyone at that table knew it. Fuck Coopa. Our allegiance lay with the head of the Last Kings. We were his soldiers, the ones who would expedite all of the missions while he handled all of the business. Ray had to have respect for everyone in that dining room otherwise they wouldn't have made it to a seat at the table. We could be out in the murderous streets of Detroit. Slanging tiny bags of coke to the neighborhood crack heads doing anything to support their habit. Instead we were a part of something much bigger. The name "Last Kings," fit perfectly as I stared at everyone around the table. We all had one thing in common I knew, we were all orphans. Sadly we were all each other had no matter how short of a time we'd known each other.

"All these businesses I'm running are cleaning this dirty money, so I don't ever want to see any of you moving on the streets," Ray's voice held not a hint of humor. Letting us all know he was serious. "That's the old way of the hustler and moving that way could jeopardize this whole operation. If I find any of you doing that I will dead you where you stand, no matter who you are. Also Coopa is expecting' that shit. Ain't none of my soldiers going to get caught slipping. So I'm about to put it to you all like this."

Ray went back to his seat at the head of the table and upon sitting down he reached under the table and pulled out seven folders. I felt Mocha lean in slightly and I saw the anticipation on her face.

"Seven kings and six businesses. It's been two months and like I said each of you have proven to me that you can pull in your own work. Now it's time for some *real* work. Each of you will manage one of my businesses."

My mind began reeling, Ray was a fucking genius, and the cartel would be run behind our businesses. Meaning there would be no dirty money. The first two months of our hustle had been building up our clientele and thanks to my idea for the club all of their names were listed. As long as we could deliver they weren't going anywhere. Ray's connect had some good shit and it was going to make us rich. I couldn't help the grin forming on my face. Wondering how long Ray had been planning it, the plan was flawless.

"My man Ty here has the fed activities in check, so if he calls you better answer your phones on the first ring. No questions asked. Sadie?" Ray turned his attention to me.

"Yes?" I inquired taking a sip of the champagne before me.

"Amore is yours," he told me and I was slightly taken aback.

Everyone sitting at the table stared at me, we all knew that not only was Amore was the Italian restaurant Ray owned but it was the heart of the whole operation. No new work would even be thought of if it didn't come through there. I definitely thought he would make Tyler the head of it. And by the expression on Tyler's face I knew our minds were thinking the same thing. Our eyes met for a moment before I averted them back to Ray.

"Ray, are you sure about that?" Tyler asked him skeptically.

It kind of set me off slightly, like he didn't think I could do it or something.

"You forget she's the reason *why* the restaurant is a big part of this whole deal," Ray told Tyler while smiling confidently at me. "I'm positive, and plus she'll have Mocha right there beside her helping' her run shit."

Tyler backed off, but I could tell he wasn't very happy with Ray's decision. I, on the other hand, felt honored that Ray had put me in such a position of power. It proved that he had trust in me beyond measures and I felt the love I had for my cousin rise. He then appointed everyone else their station. Tyler would head the chain of laundry mats, Devynn was put head of the hair salon, D was set up to be the landlord of the apartment buildings, Adrianna would manage the nightclub Lace, and Amann was entrusted with the convenient store Ray had recently purchased. Ray slid a folder in front of each of us. I opened mine and noticed that it contained the blueprints of Amore with several escape routes.

"You will all learn the blueprints the buildings; a boss is never caught slipping in his own place of business. There are undetectable stash spots in every building, learn them. There are also artillery rooms in every building, keep them stocked," Ray told us. "This is the last movement Detroit will ever see."

"The Last Kings," I felt that that was the right moment to raise my glass and everyone else followed suit.

"The Last Kings!" They all said in unison, but before we could drink our toast I noticed a red dot slowly moving to the center of Mocha's forehead.

Before I knew what was going on instinct took over and I pushed Mocha out of her chair. No sooner had she hit the ground did the glass patio door shatter and a bullet hit the wall behind where Mocha was sitting. After that first bullet it seemed as though hundreds more followed.

Everyone was caught off guard as we saw at least fifteen hooded masked figures in all black appear in the backyard shooting rogue bullets into Ray's home.

"They found us!" Tyler yelled and we all ducked trying to dodge bullets.

Devynn and Adrianna pulled out their burners in a matter of seconds and began shooting expertly at the advancing enemy. I watched the first few fall after their heads exploded before pulling out my own pistol preparing to take a few out myself. Before I could get my first shot off Ray grabbed my arm preventing me from standing to my feet.

"Get to the garage!" Ray ordered to Mocha and I as popped two niggas trying to get through the patio door.

I snatched my arm from him.

"Fuck that!" I stared at Mocha who was frozen on the ground in shock and fear not knowing what to do. "It's ok." I whispered to her.

Just as the words left my mouth I heard noise coming from the living room and looked up in time to see a hooded figure aiming for our two bodies on the ground. I quickly pointed my gun at him and put two neat holes in his dome causing him to slow the three coming up from behind him down. It gave Mocha and me time to stand to our feet and dead them where they stood. What was supposed to be a simple business meeting had turned into a battlefield. There were bullets whizzing past my head left and right, God must have had my back because I didn't even feel a graze. We were clearly outnumbered, but in their case strength didn't come in numbers. They were sloppy and it was obvious with their bodies piling that they hadn't thought their plan all the way through.

"You wanna play huh? You wanna play bitch!" I heard Adrianna's rants as she clicked heartlessly on the intruders.

"These muhfuckas is sad yo!" Devynn actually laughed as she put five bullets in one body and reloaded taking cover behind Adrianna.

From nowhere I heard the sound of automatic rounds being let out and I knew for sure that we were all goners, but then I saw that it was D and Amann. Both were toting AK 47's and they finished the last of the intruders off. When the blazing stopped all of our guns were smoking and Ray's house, usually spotless and tidy. There was a bloodbath with at least twenty dead bodies. One of them was still moving, trying to crawl away. He was closest to me so I walked up behind him placing my foot on his back. He grunted at the pain of the weight of my foot and the bullets caused blood to spill from his body. Bending down I snatched the mask from his face and instantly recognized him as Antwan, Mocha's old boo. Ray smiled and shook his head knowing Antwan's connection to Coopa.

"Your man sent you to my home to dead me?" Ray walked up to him and kicked him in his face so hard I saw a few teeth slide along the stained red carpet. "I would have you give that nigga a message for me...but your body in a duffle bag should do just fine.

Ray raised his gun slightly and put a bullet in each of Antwan's eye sockets.

"Bitch nigga," Ray spat. "We have to move, I know the neighbors heard all that shit. I also know that if none of his men return to tell him the job he sent them on is done he's going to send another sweep in. Get a cleaner team here in two point five Tyler. Adrianna; take Mocha and Sadie somewhere to lay their heads for the night. The rest of you know what to do. Hit the block, find this nigga. This nigga sent these pussy ass muhfucka's to my house? This is war."

Ray was barking orders before it registered in anyone's head what had just happened. His gangster shone as he was never knocked off his A game, no matter the situation.

"I'm not leaving you," I told my cousin worried about him.

Ray had been wrong; he thought Coopa wouldn't try him. The scene there proved that Coopa was taking Ray's come up to the heart and wanted him out of the game bad. So bad that he hadn't even thought thoroughly about his plan of action. All his niggas lay dead, their souls floating above us. If Coopa was that clouded by anger there was no telling what his next malicious act would be. I refused to leave my cousin's side.

"Sadie this isn't something to negotiate," Ray told me his voice slightly soft. He knew I was worried and he hugged me handing Adrianna a wad of hundreds. "Take my bullet proof Hummer, and park it somewhere lowkey. I'll call you in the morning."

Adrianna nodded her head knowing that protecting Mocha and I was her job.

"Let's go," she instructed a little forcefully and grabbed us by the arms.

"Ray!" I called back at him not able to break away from Adrianna's tight grip on my arm.

"I'll call in the morning," Ray promised again.

"Sadie it's going to be ok, for now we need to listen to Ray," Mocha told me.

I obliged and with one last look at my cousin's enraged face I followed Adrianna to refuge sand out of harm's way

♟ CHAPTER 10

After a while it seemed to Ray that Coopa was an invisible man. After the fiasco at Ray's home Coopa had doubled up on his protection. He had decoys for days and stayed at least twenty deep wherever he went. Coopa was playing it safe, when the bodies of the dead were delivered at his front door. He knew that Ray was not someone to take lightly. Something he honestly should have known from working with him for years. Coopa had watched Ray's rise but hadn't paid enough attention to it because out of all of Coopa's goons Ray was always the least flashy. Ray didn't have slew of bitches or baby mamas and he wasn't tricking off. Coopa knew then when it was too late that he should have wondered what Ray was doing with all of his money. Stacking up was what he was doing and when Coopa caught wind of an underground movement happening in his city he flipped. He was even more angered when he learned through the street vine that Ray was the head of the whole operation. When he sent his goons to move in on Ray he had underestimated the strength of Ray's little army. He thought for sure they would be killed in Ray's home and he would just go back to running Detroit with an iron fist the next day. How wrong had he been, none of his men made it home to their families and he was to blame for that. But that was the least of his worries; he only cared about his own well being. He'd seen firsthand how Ray got down. His aim was flawless. It was the reason he wanted him on his team in the first place. Coopa knew that with a murderer like Ray he needed the extra protection and being caught slipping would most definitely cost him his life. He stayed low, sending his most loyal men to handle his business. There was a big drop coming up and he knew that his empire couldn't risk the loss of the possible new connect. JoJo, Coopa's new right hand man, was sent in Coopa's place to the Italian restaurant Amore and was expected to conduct business on Coopa's behalf. Coopa heard that some big time Italian muhfucka had some kill. He knew if he got that I his streets they would have what they had been crying for. Coopa wasn't stupid; he could see his streets getting hungry. At first he didn't care as long as he was still on top. But it didn't take long for niggas to turn and think they would get away with hitting licks on his trap houses. Coopa had to turn things around because he would rather drink piss than kneel at the feet of a nigga *he* put on.

Ray wanted to move on Coopa but refused to let anger cloud his judgment. He knew Coopa wasn't going to be stupid enough to come directly at him again, so he felt comfortable in his position. Business would have to continue, The Last Kings were only at the beginning of their rise. Ray sat in the back of Amore awaiting the arrival of a new potential client. Although Vinny was just the connect he felt a strange draw to Ray. He had been in the world of cocaine all of his life and it was rare to see things change for the better. He knew from the first day of speaking to Ray that he would bring something to the game that had never been done before. Ray and

Vinny spoke often and he dealt his hand in Ray's business, he wanted Ray's operation to succeed. When Ray told him about everything that was going on he could have easily taken Coopa out of the game, one hit. But he knew that this was something Ray must do on his own to earn his right of passage to the throne. He knew Ray's eyes were on the prize, Detroit. He also knew that Coopa knew the city like the back of his hand. Meaning touching him would be almost impossible; almost. Since Vinny touched down in Detroit Coopa had been trying to make contact, but Vinny didn't want to give him his business. He felt he was too incompetent and foolish to push his work. Vinny made a phone call and set the meeting up; knowing that no one in the city knew about Ray and his connection. He rolled the dice; it was up to Ray to determine what they landed on.

A man wearing Ralph Lauren cargo shorts and a blue Ralph Lauren polo entered Amore. Although he wore sunglasses to shield his eyes Ray recognized him as a man he had put in a lot of work with. JoJo glanced around the restaurant trying to spot his contact and Ray quickly stood up as a waiter passed, walking at his pace to shield his body. Once he made it into the kitchen that was the size of a small house he walked quickly to the secret entrance of the club. He thought quickly, JoJo was there to conduct business which meant Coopa clearly couldn't have known that Ray was his contact. Ray couldn't let JoJo see him; he had to find a new connect. Sadie and Mocha were automatically out of the equation, everyone knew their connection with Ray. Plus he had them handling a major deal at that time. D and Amman were out making a few drops and Devynn just didn't fit the role. When Ray stepped foot in the dimmed lighting of the club he walked the long hallway in search for Adrianna. He had to find her quickly before JoJo thought it was a setup and left. Ray passed several rooms. Each had a valuable customer testing his product to ecstasy.

He found Adrianna in the Money Room counting and bagging. When she saw Ray she smiled very sexy up at him. Her smile was flawless and she wet her lips with her tongue. She wore her long silky brunette hair in a ponytail and her attraction to him read easily on her face, but her actions spoke another story. She was a woman scorned and she didn't want to get involved emotionally with another hustler. She knew it wasn't forever. After being the ride or die bitch for two of the big time hustlers and watching one get tortured and killed and the other's brains blown out she decided that she would only be in the game to make her money. Not for love, but being in Ray's presence proved to be difficult. He was different than any other man she'd ever encountered.

The rising attraction Adrianna was feeling for Ray was definitely mutual. Shorty was bad and Ray knew she knew it. Ray was attracted to her ruthless swagger. She wasn't afraid to die nor was she afraid to kill an enemy. She was the type of bitch who rode shot gun, with a shot gun. Ray saw more than the image she tried to spit out for others to see, he saw way deeper than that. He read her pain easily only because she hid it so well. Adrianna was really just a soft bluff. The way Adrianna looked at him, Ray knew it was best not to get involved. It was clear that he already had one soft spot, Saidee, and mixing business with pleasure was never a good thing. Ray knew that if he allowed himself to get too close to Adrianna he would get too attached and love got you killed and in Adrianna's case she knew that too well. For now Ray knew that business was all that could be between him and Adrianna.

"I need you," Ray started and instantly saw Adrianna's face brighten. "Chill ma," Ray said not wanting to give her the wrong idea. "Business as usual."

Adrianna's face dropped and she rolled her eyes. She wasn't going to lie, she was disappointed. It was random of Ray to just pop up on her and a little piece of her was hoping he wanted to lay her down on the counting table and have his way with her.

"What's up, *boss*?" She asked putting extra emphasis on her last word in sarcasm.

She didn't mind Ray keeping her at a respectable distance. It made her urges easier to keep under control. The old Adrianna would have gotten at Ray quickly and easily, but Adrianna had left the "wifey" life behind. Ray briefed her on the situation and before he even finished telling her the plan she was down to ride.

"'Aight," Adrianna nodded her head, her New York accent thick. She threw the remaining money stacks into a duffle bag and stood up. "Dude is upstairs now?"

Ray nodded his head.

"Yea shorty," he looked her up and down determining then that what she was wearing was sexy enough to entice JoJo's tiny brain.

Adrianna was looking quite edible wearing a Diamond Supply hoodie with red embroidery that fit snugly on her upper half. The Levi jeggings she wore hugged her wide hips just right and Ray couldn't help but to notice how beautiful she was. Her almond colored skin seemed to glow. She wore her hair pulled back allowing her high cheekbones and bright round hazel eyes to be very distinguishable. With her full lips and plump breasts she was what most would call a bad bitch.

"Aye ma, you got this hard chick act going' on. I need you to sexy it up a little for me," Ray instructed. "Take them sneakers off; Mocha has a pair of Red Bottoms in that cabinet over there. Put them on and let's go to work."

Adrianna nodded her head pleased with the look of lust she saw in Ray's eyes. It was only there for a split second as he eyed her body, but she caught it.

"Don't worry papi, I got this," Adrianna said sincerely putting the pumps on her feet.

She pulled the ponytail holder out of her hair letting it fall in soft curls around her face. Winking at Ray; she led the way to the restaurant. Her job was simple, flirt with JoJo, make a deal, and then get him to come home with her...well to a hotel room that evening. Ray knew JoJo was his key to Coopa and he couldn't fuck it up. With JoJo's long list of baby mama's Ray knew that all he needed was a little liquor in his system for him to take the bait.

"Don't fuck up ma," Ray said briefly grabbing her arm.

Adrianna paused before stepping through the secret door that lead into the kitchen of the restaurant.

"Like I said, I got this," she gently removed her arm from his grip and smirked. "Don't get jealous."

Ray smiled as he watched her sashay away. He didn't doubt her for a moment.

* * *

Adrianna walked seductively to the king sized bed inside of the bedroom in the hotel suite. The lights were dimmed and Trey Songz was playing softly in the background. All it took were a few shots of Hennessey in his system and he was ready to jump her bones.

This is who Coopa has working' his fucking' team? Fuckin' pathetic! Adrianna thought disgustedly smiling at JoJo who lay naked on the bed.

She wore a sexy red bra and thong set and with every little movement her ass jiggled a little bit. She was used to men going crazy over her frame and her smooth almond skin so the hungry expression on JoJo's face was nothing new to her. She wanted to laugh. One because he was ugly as fuck and black, and two because she wondered exactly what the fuck he thought he was going to do with his tiny 5 inch penis. Dancing seductively towards him she turned around and began making her round ass cheeks clap.

"You want me daddy?" she whispered.

JoJo's eyes were glued to the two saucers before them; all he could do was nod his answer.

"Good," she licked her lips and proceeded to crawl up the bed until she was directly over him. "How do you want me?"

"Just like this baby," JoJo gripped both of her cheeks tightly, one in each hand.

Adrianna giggled and positioned herself over him. She began teasing him by grinding on his hardness, letting him feel her wetness. JoJo threw his head back in pleasure.

"Damn ma! I can't wait to dive into this shit, fuck!"

Adrianna laughed knowing he would never dive into anything ever again except a grave. She placed her hands on his and removed them from her cheeks and then slid them up the bed above his head. Her body was positioned in an arc and her knees on the side of his hips. She looked into his thirsty eyes and smiled slyly before yelling,

"Now!"

On cue Ray entered the hotel room with the key Adrianna had snuck to him when JoJo made a dash to the restroom.

"What the fuck?" JoJo exclaimed seeing the raised gun pointing at him

"What up JoJo!" Ray smirked at the pussy ass nigga before him.

He walked over to where Adrianna had undressed JoJo. Taking notice of how luscious Adrianna looked in her lingerie he kicked JoJo's clothes to the side.

"You have thirty seconds to tell me where Coopa is," Ray cocked his gun allowing Adrianna time to climb off of the bed.

"Ray man —" before JoJo could get the words out of his mouth he had a bullet in his leg.

"Twenty seconds," Ray said as blood spilled all over the bed from JoJo's oozing leg.

"Ray please," JoJo said seeing his life flash before his eyes. "I don't know where that nigga is!"

Ray shot his gun again, the silencer made a soft *PFT* as a bullet caught JoJo in his torso.

"Ten seconds," Ray said coldly aiming his gun at the thing JoJo definitely didn't want to lose. He wasn't there to talk or to listen to a begging ass nigga.

"Ahh!" JoJo breathed heavily trying to cradle his wounds. That didn't stop him from talking shit. "Fuck you nigga! You ain't shit but what Coopa made you, *nothing*. I ain't no snake ass nigga like you pussy! You're trying to take something that ain't yours nigga. Did you think war wasn't going to break out? Coopa is going to dead ya ass bro."

Ray laughed at JoJo's words, knowing that he was just a dead man talking. He wanted to see how much about his words JoJo really was. Ray cocked his gun and shot a bullet so close to JoJo's penis although he made sure he didn't hit it. JoJo let out a scream so loud Ray would have sworn a little girl was somewhere hiding in the room and just like the chicken Ray knew he was he began clucking out information.

"That nigga said he had business to attend to, you may actually know about it," JoJo was breathing rigid but still managed to let out a sick smile. "Morgan Towers ring a bell?"

A red flag went up in Ray's head and Adrianna looked at him already knowing what was wrong. Morgan Towers was where Mocha and Sadie had set out to make a deal with one of their usual customers. It was a rundown apartment building. He rented out an apartment there to do some of his major deals. It was a perfect spot just because it was so obvious and he'd been using it for years. He'd been using it for so long he should have known that Coopa would have caught wind at what exactly took place there. JoJo began laughing controllably.

"You can kill me now," he said blood trickling down the side of his mouth. "But ya cousin will be joining me soon."

He still had a smile on his face when Ray lit his body up with the rest of his clip.

"Bitch," Ray spat on his dead body.

"Ray we have to go!" Adrianna said already fully dressed. She grabbed her clutch purse and ran for the door.

Ray began trying to get a hold of Sadie by calling her cell phone but it just went straight to voicemail. Same with Mocha.

"Fuck!" Ray exclaimed as they ran through the hotel trying to make it to the exit.

Adrianna saw the worry all over Ray's face. She couldn't lie and say she wasn't worried too. If Coopa had gone himself to where Sadie and Mocha were to make a drop nothing good could come out of it. Coopa was a weak leader, but she knew how merciless of a killer he was. Adrianna knew that Saidee and Mocha were inexperienced when it came to the murder game. She hoped that they wouldn't become victims.

Please let us get there in time, Adrianna said a silent prayer hopping into Ray's Escalade. They hit eighty across town knowing that two of their own' lives were on a countdown.

♟ CHAPTER 11

M ocha and I entered the apartment with the key Ray had given me. Larry, the guy Ray had sent us to meet was supposed to be in the living room waiting for us. It was supposed to be a simple pick up, not more than five minutes. But As soon as I stepped foot in the two bedroom apartment I knew that walking back out might not have been an option that we had. Mocha inhaled sharply when she saw Larry's body lying face down on the carpeted floor, a pool of blood formed neatly around his head.

"Sadie," Mocha started but never finished.

Four men made their presence known walking from the back rooms, they all had their guns drawn. My heart stopped when I recognized one of the men as none other than Coopa. My mind wrapped around what the fuck was happening. Coopa had to have set us up and I felt my heart twist into knots. Coopa stared coldly at the two of us standing there.

"Some bitches?" He eyed us up and down and laughed. "This is how Ray conducts his business?"

Coopa was a good looking light skinned older man, but the way his face was always turned up took the handsome out of his appearance. He kept his head cut bald, probably because he was balding up top and the goatee on his face was neatly trimmed. He stood before us at six foot two in a tan Armani suit with the matching shoes. Coopa motioned for his men to check us, which they did gladly removing every weapon we had on our bodies but they left my clutch in my hands. When they were done Coopa began to pace slowly in front of us.

"I heard through the grape vine that there was a new operation starting in Detroit and I thought 'Nah not my city!' Don't know work come through this muhfucka if I don't know about it! Imagine my shock when I found out Ray was the snake going' under my nose trying to take what's mine!" He waived his hands to the duffle bags of money on the couch that contained the two hundred and fifty thousand we were there to pick up. "Look at this shit! Two hundred and fifty stacks I would have been missing out on...do you see the error in this fuckin equation? That's *my* fucking money! Mine!"

Coopa stopped pacing to stand directly in front of me and looked into my eyes. He grabbed my face and, squeezing hard, pulled it close to his. At that moment, seeing the lust in his eyes, I regretted wearing my skinny Miss Me jeans with only a green tank top. The weather was nice, I didn't expect to have to dress to get robbed. I smelled his scent and knew that too had to be an Armani fragrance, hating how nice it was I tried to turn away. I caught a glimpse of Mocha and admired the hardened look she had on her face. I knew she was terrified and I immediately was consumed with guilt knowing it was my fault she was in that predicament in the first place. She looked back at me and gave me a look that said everything would be ok, like she knew exactly what I was thinking. Her head was held high as the men around her tried to spook her with their guns.

They'd gotten me for all of my weapons except for one. I had a 22 magnum revolver in my clutch loaded and ready to bust at the right moment. Coopa surprised me by grabbing my ass harder than anyone ever had.

"Don't fucking touch me," I glared at Coopa trying to push him away from me.

I didn't give a fuck about the guns pointed my way anymore. I didn't like the way Coopa was licking his lips at me. Flash backs of Nino began popping up in my head and I wanted nothing more but for them all to be erased.

"Bitch!" Coopa snatched me up by my neck so fast I barely had time to take a breath. "You working for this nigga who's stealing from me *and* you his fam. You're about to pay a small part of his debt to me!"

Mocha dashed over to where Coopa had me and jumped on his back beating him with her fists.

"Get the fuck off of her!" She screamed and bit his ear like Mike Tyson.

Coopa yelled in pain before he got control and flung her off of his back.

"Get that bitch!" He directed his henchmen. "One of you should have shot her!"

One of the men, a fat dark skinned man who probably got no pussy, grabbed for Mocha but she swung and connected with his jaw. The slap he landed on her face was so brutal the sound echoed throughout the apartment.

"Mocha!" I screamed trying to push Coopa off of me.

I saw blood trickling down Mocha's nose and wanted to get over to where she was. Coopa laughed at

THE LAST KINGS

my feeble attempts knowing I couldn't over power him. He picked me up and carried me to one of the bedrooms in the back. No matter how much I kicked or screamed I couldn't get free. Coopa tossed me on the bed in the master bedroom like a pillow and locked the door behind him. I wanted to cry hearing Mocha's spine tingling screams of my name over and over.

"No point in trying to run ma," Coopa grabbed my Fendi clutch and threw it to the side of the bed.

The soft thud it made was slightly noticeable but Coopa paid it no mind. He was too busy forcing my pants off. I spat on him.

"I'm going to kill you," I snarled in an icy tone.

I sounded so confident that he fumbled with my pants a bit. He regained his composure quickly as he pulled a handkerchief from the pocket of his suit jacket. I knew that Coopa, like Nino years before, was going to take something that I would never willingly give to him. Chuckling Coopa threw the handkerchief to the side and gave me his pearly white smile.

"Feisty! And you got a fat ass," he winked at me. "This should be fun."

Coopa then removed his pants and jacket. In those few moments I made the decision to not fight it. Every odd was against me and my goal was to get to my clutch, the prize lay inside it. Coopa was slipping by letting me stay alive longer than necessary to get his self-proclaimed money. I closed my eyes and tried not to think about the fact that once again my womanhood was getting stolen once again. I took a deep breath and made a decision. I was going to put on a good show and then let a round off into his big ass head. I opened my legs allowing Coopa to have all access to me and a pleased look spread across his face.

"If you're going to kill me anyways I might as well enjoy this shit," I told him playing with my pearl.

Coopa licked his lips as he watched my panties moisten.

"Damn shorty," Coopa said kissing my inner thigh.

He moved my panties to one side and let his tongue explore the depths of my treasure. My hands ran over his smooth head as I relished in the feeling of his warm tongue slipping and sliding tasting my sweet nectar. A few moans escaped my mouth and he stopped suddenly shaking his head.

"This shit it too wet, turn around let me get this pussy from the back," Coopa said.

I must have been going too slow because he grabbed my ankles and flipped me over himself putting me at a perfect angle on the queen sized bed to reach down and grab my clutch.

Ok Sadie now you just have to play your fucking cards right, I thought knowing the ball was in my court.

The feeling of Coopa ramming his monster all up inside of me interrupted my thoughts. My walls instinctively clenched tightly. Coopa proceeded to beat my love spot into ecstasy. He was giving it to me so good I even began throwing it back at him. I looked back at him and saw how infatuated he was with my ass.

"Damn ma, you got a fat ass fuck! Why you have to be that nigga's people? I could've made you my shorty!" Coopa threw his head back while he rode me until I felt myself about to explode.

"Fuck I'm about to cuuuuuum!" I couldn't help crying out.

I couldn't hold back anymore and my body quivered violently with the intensity of my orgasm. Coopa had my juices dripping all over him but he still wasn't ready to bust.

Fuck, I have to get this nigga to nut! I thought.

I started to make my ass clap as I threw it back at him hoping that would be enough to make him bust.

"Hell yea take this dick! Oooh shit!" Coopa gripped my hips tightly and I finally felt his dick pulsating inside of me. "I'm about to...ahhh!"

Coopa pulled out of me and squirted what seemed like a gallon of semen onto the bed. While he was busy enjoying the feel of his nut I used that as my window of opportunity to reach down and grab my clutch. Although my legs were shaking and I could barely stand I knew what had to be done.

"Well bitch it was fun," Coopa wiped his hands on the bed sheets and reached for the .45 he must have set on the ground while he was fucking me. "It's a shame I have to kill you now."

The second he took his eyes off me to grab his gun was the second I used to aim mine. I let one round off catching him in the arm and by surprise. The force of my bullet caused him to drop his gun and fumble back.

"Ahh!" Coopa cringed gripping his arm in pain. "Bitch!"

"The fuck did you think was going to happen here?" I said standing there in just my panties and tank top. "Did you think you were going to fuck me, kill us, *rob* us, and live to tell the fuckin' tale?"

I let out a crazed laugh at the sight of Coopa standing there weighing his options. He knew he'd lost and the realization he was feeling made me happy.

"Nigga I'm a Last King! We don't fuckin' die!" I raised my gun again feeling the power in my words. "You know what your mistake was Coopa? You got too *fuckin'* comfortable and the streets got hungry. We're here because you lost your boss mentality and because of you Detroit seems weak. We're here because you failed to do your job, but I guess it's good that we're here to take your place. Huh?"

Coopa tried desperately to make a quick grab for the gun around his ankle but I pulled the trigger one more time rocking him to sleep forever.

"Bitch," I spat and kicked his dead body.

After I put my pants back on I opened the door to the bedroom as quietly as I could. The television in the living room was on loudly, that explained why they didn't hear the bullets that had just killed their boss.

"Stop!" I heard Mocha cry out over the television and snickers in the background as I eased closer to the living room. "Get the fuck off me you dirty dick ass niggas!"

I closed my eyes quickly trying to envision who all was in the room. There was one big black nigga and two fair skinned skinny niggas. From their movements I could tell that they were all in one area of the living room. I knew they were strapped, but I didn't give a fuck. I would take many bullets for Mocha if they hurt a hair on her head. I took a deep breath and entered the room gun raised. As soon as I was seen enter the room my finger clicked the trigger catching one of the skinny guys in the chest. He dropped like a fly. They'd been in the middle of trying to pin Mocha down and pry her legs open. The turquoise Fendi dress that she'd decided to wear would have given them easy access, but from the looks of it they were having a pretty tough time.

"What the—" The big one started.

"Fuck?" I finished for him and cold bloodedly splattered his brains throughout the room with two bullets.

His fat ass needed two bullets to send him to the afterlife. I felt a bullet whiz past my head and saw that the last guy had time enough to get a shot off. However Mocha kicked him throwing off his aim. She then pulled her hidden pistol from her thigh and emptied the clip into his head. When she was done his head was no longer on his body, instead it was in little pieces scattered everywhere in the room.

"Stupid bitch!" Mocha kicked the bodies of the fallen as her body shook uncontrollably.

She made her way to where I stood and embraced me. She pulled back and examined me.

"Did he—"

"Yes," I answered her truthfully before the question fully formed from her mouth.

"Are you—" she stared again.

"I'm fine," I told her walking to the couch and grabbing one of the two duffle bags of drug money. "Grab that shit, we gotta go."

Mocha understood that it wasn't the time or the place to get sentimental and obliged to my orders. I grabbed everything they'd taken from us and noticed I had a shit load of missed calls, all from Ray and Adrianna. I was about to call Ray back when Mocha and I rushed out of the apartment building but just as I hit the last number I saw Ray's Escalade pull in front of the building. Ray jumped quickly from the driver's side and rushed to us.

"Say you cool? Y'all good?" He asked worry drenched my cousin's handsome face

I embraced my cousin tightly to let him know that I was all good. When I pulled back I looked into his eyes and smirked lightly.

"Go see for yourself," I told him throwing the duffle bag into the back of his truck.

Nodding my head to the apartment I stepped out of the way so Ray could go check out the murder scene. Adrianna, who'd been making sure Mocha was ok, quickly followed suit wanting to see what had gone down. When Ray came back out he wore a huge grin on his face and I knew he was pleased with the death of Detroit's old kingpin.

"Straight like that?" Ray asked extending his hand.

I nodded my head and shook his hand grinning.

"Like that."

Ray's grin slowly turned into a frown as he stared into my eyes.

"That nigga ain't have no pants on Say," his eyes pierced into mine but I couldn't look away. "What the fuck happened up there?"

I knew he would be scoping for a lie and I couldn't tell him what really happened. I could already see guilt forming on his face. He was blaming himself for the whole ordeal. I thought carefully about my words before delivering a story. I glanced at Mocha as if to say *"Go along with this shit,"* before I started speaking.

"As soon as Mocha and I walked in it was on and popping. They off'd our man before we even got there. Coopa was talking' beef shit and was planning' on taken' the money after he did what he wanted with me," I took a breath before I continued seeing the vein slowly throbbing on his temple. "He took me to the back room and he had three other nigga's there making' sure Mocha's ass ain't go nowhere."

"They unstrapped you?" Ray asked.

"Yea, but the dumb nigga never took my clutch," I told him.

Ray shook his head at Coopa's stupidity.

"As soon as he dropped his pants I pulled my gun out and blasted his ass," I tasted salt as the lie rolled off of my tongue. "Then we finished the niggas off in the living room. This murder shit is pretty gangster, I could get used to this."

Despite the fact that we'd almost died Mocha stifled a laugh at my joke but Ray stood firm and serious.

"This ain't shit to joke about Sadie! I should have never sent you to handle this shit! That nigga thought he was smart, you could have fuckin' died and—"

"But I didn't!" I reassured my cousin. "Kings don't die, they live on forever."

Ray looked lovingly into my eyes and I knew why he was tripping' so hard. We grew up with only each other, until Mocha came along. If anything happened to me I knew Ray would go insane and vice versa. He nodded his head agreeing with my words.

"You right. Kings don't die, the important thing is that bitch nigga is finally out of the picture," Ray grabbed the duffle bag from Mocha and handed it to Adrianna.

Coopa and Adrianna got into his Escalade to take the money to where it was supposed to go. He instructed us to go directly back to his penthouse and wait for him there. Mocha and I got into her BMW 335i. I knew a sweeper team would be there soon to clean up the mess and take Coopa's body to his home front. The message would be clear. Coopa's reign was dead. The time of The Last Kings were amongst Detroit. It was time to make our official claim on the city.

♟ CHAPTER 12

Two Years Later

After Coopa's death the rise of Last Kings had to be swift and accurate. There wasn't any room for fuck ups. The feds were all over Coopa's operation after his body was found. The majority of his soldiers weren't prepared to answer questions and explain where the drug money came from. They took Ray in for questioning of course because at one point in time he and Coopa were clearly were in cahoots. But they didn't have enough on him to keep him in custody; the murder weapon was never found. If they would have even tried to hold him, he had more than enough money to get out. So they just let him go. They couldn't tie him to the murder or to the drugs and money found in Coopa's traps but Ray knew he would have to tread soft for a while. In the streets at least.

Mocha switched her way into Lace wearing a skin tight Armani one strap dress that stopped just above her knee and holding a clutch and a black folder in her hands. The sleek black of the dress clung to her body giving the illusion that it was actually painted on. She stepped through the door not even bothering to flash the guard the tattoo of the pharaoh on her forearm, he knew she was affiliated. Mocha smirked as he watched her step, catching every quake of her ass.

You ain't never going to taste this boo, Mocha thought to herself as she made her way through the dim lighting of the strip club to the back. It wasn't too busy, there was a nice crowd surrounding the stage watching the hoes twirl around on the poles.

The stairwell led to the locker room for the strippers. Mocha knew better she wasn't going there to chill with any of those hoes. She walked past many naked women preparing for their acts and headed directly for the showers and bathroom stalls. The last stall was handicapped and on the door it read "Out Of Order" but Mocha entered it anyways. She pulled a set of keys from her clutch purse and opened the tampon contractor that was on the wall above the toilet paper. Instead of tampons inside it there was a keypad in which Mocha entered a code that consisted of six numbers. Once the last number was entered she heard a soft click and light hum. Before her the concrete wall the toilet was attached too opened just a crack, enough for her to reach her hand through and open it the rest of the way. She walked through it entering the secret and only trap house of The Last Kings. Ray had learned from Coopa's mistakes and knew the location of his trap had to be ducked off and out of the way. Mocha walked down one more flight of stairs before entering a long hallway. At the end of the hallway was a tall door and on the outside of it two big niggas stood guard. They opened the door for her before she'd even gotten all the way to them and she nodded when she walked through. Almost immediately she was hit with the aroma of cocaine being cut up and bagged before she saw the bitches in Victoria's Secret lingerie dealing with the product. Making sure it was cut and bagged correctly. They wore masks over their mouths and noses to protect them from the debris and in front of each of them on the tables lay a pistol. Mocha didn't even acknowledge the bitches and went to the back room. She'd just made a big business investment and she had come to wrap up some loose ends with Tyler. She opened the door to the basement and traveled down the stairs to where she knew Tyler were.

"Gotta show these niggas that fear don't live in ya fucking hearts," Tyler was instructing a room full of young men. "These niggas think we can be touched just because Coopa got murked, fuck that!" He went and grabbed one of the young men's arms and held it up showing everyone the tattoo of a pyramid he had on his forearm. "This is who the fuck we are! What we do is make this money, branded for life; one way in, one way out. If you got this fuckin tattoo that means you're in this shit forever. We are family, y'all not just soldiers. But cross this team and I will put a hollow tip in ya fucking head like you was just some random muhfucka on the street. Ya' hearing me?"

Mocha stood back listening to Tyler's speech that he was giving and noticed Adrianna and Devynn standing behind him. Mocha knew that anyone in that room had to be a cold blooded killer, they couldn't afford to have any bitch niggas on their team. Bitch niggas were the same as snitch niggas and the Last Kings were allergic to those. Leaning on the wall Mocha admired the respect that was held in the room. A nigga would have to be a fool if he didn't respect Tyler. It was true he was a loose cannon but if you showed loyalty to him then he would be loyal to you.

This is really us, she thought pleased looking at the hungry looks of the niggas in the room. It was a fact that she was very skeptical about the whole operation, she wasn't a killer. At least that's what she thought before she pulled the trigger of her new found best friend. It was surprising to her how easily she could take a life, the money was the motive and if a body was in her way...well. Tyler noticed Mocha standing behind the crowd of niggas in the room and dismissed them all.

"What's up ma?" Tyler said coming up on her. His hair was freshly cut into a fade and his facial hair was neatly trimmed. He wore Ralph Lauren from head to toe. The Rolex and diamonds shining from his ears let off that he was straight hood even though he carried himself like royalty.

Mocha smiled at her business partner seeing the imprint of the .45 through his shirt.

"Kings stay strapped at all times, even in his own house," Ray always said.

"Business as usual, don't act brand new Tyler," she told him rolling her eyes slightly. He knew that would be the only reason she would even come to the trap. "Where's Ray?"

"That nigga is handling' business as usual," Tyler smirked having fun being an asshole to Mocha who had become like a little sister to him. "What you got for us though shorty?"

Mocha was slightly disappointed that Ray wasn't there. She wanted to see the pleased look on his face when she told him they'd come up on two hundred thousand dollars. She liked when he looked at her the same he did Sadie. The only difference was that Sadie didn't have to do anything to get that look. Ray was proud of her regardless. Mocha often felt tiny pings of jealousy when it came to their relationship. Although they only had each other and Grandma Rae that was more family than she'd ever had. Mocha's mother forced her to move from Atlanta in junior high and then left her when she was in high school. She sent her to school with a note that said

I ain't coming' back for this little bitch, y'all can keep her!

That was when Grandma Rae had taken her in. Sadie didn't even have to ask her and Grandma Rae acted as if Mocha had been staying there all her life. Mocha knew she had no reason to feel that green bitch especially when Ray did everything in his power to make her feel at home. If she needed anything he had her and she loved him like the big brother she never had.

"Nothing' much, just made a deal that's all," she handed him the red folder she had in her hands with the details of the drop to be made.

"Damn shorty! Two hundred stacks!" Tyler said obviously pleased. "That's real nigga shit."

He grinned down at Mocha causing her skin to blush a bit. She shrugged her shoulders as if to say, "It was nothing."

Tyler was sexy. No, Tyler was sexy as fuck. But she wouldn't dare try and get his attention for three reasons. Tyler was a loose cannon, which was the reason he was perfect for the job of Ray's general. He thought with his trigger finger and his body pile had added up quite drastically over the years. He was ruthless and mercy was something that he knew nothing about, so it was impossible to show it. The second reason, although she thought Mocha didn't know, Sadie had some type of feelings towards him. Mocha didn't know what had happened but she knew for a while when they were in high school all Sadie spoke about was Tyler. But then one day it just stopped. Sadie never spoke about it and since then the way she was with Tyler was different. Even now Sadie kept everything strictly business with him, but Mocha didn't press for details. Her girl had the right to her privacy just like she did. The last reason was because she had a love interest already. And she wasn't thinking about any other nigga.

"I had to bring something big in, since I'm going to be gone for a minute," she told him.

"Where you going? Atlanta again?" Tyler asked knowingly.

Mocha nodded her head.

"Yea, I've just been feeling a little home sick that's all," she lied through her teeth.

Tyler however didn't catch her lie instead closed the folder in his hands letting her know that as soon as Ray made it in he would have him handle that.

"Cool, stay up," she said and prepared to make her departure. She raised her arm that had the Last King brand that only she, Tyler, Ray, and Sadie had. Tyler raised the same arm in farewell and with that Mocha exited the basement.

She checked her watch as soon as she was back into her BMW and saw she only had four hours until her flight to Atlanta.

"Fuck!" she said aloud not wanting to miss the only connection she had to her love.

She hadn't told anyone the real reason why she'd been taking so many trips to Atlanta. She couldn't tell Sadie, she wouldn't understand why she hadn't told her about him after all the time that had passed. Mocha had been seeing him ever since her field trip to an Atlanta college campus when the two were still in college. She smiled as she reflected on her first meeting with Khiron...

"This club is wack!" Mocha whined to Jaylin who was supposed to be showing her a good time and not boring her.

Mocha was from Atlanta so she knew something had to be wrong if the club wasn't popping.

"That's because the party isn't here yet, now chill and enjoy this drink that old nigga bought for you!" Jaylin said laughing acknowledging the drink in front of Mocha. The man who sent it tipped his hat at them and the both fell into a fit of giggles.

Jaylin was cool people and upon their first greeting in the dorm room she and Mocha shared. Mocha knew she could fuck with her all day. She was two years older than Mocha and quickly took her under her wing. Like Mocha Jaylin was known to turn heads. Her chocolate skin, natural curls, and wide hips made it hard to miss her. When she walked by all eyes were on her ass and drool was likely to hit the floor. She had the looks of a model standing at 5'7 she was probably the baddest bitch on her campus. She scoped Mocha out based off of her looks and decided that she'd ever seen a woman more beautiful, not even herself. She knew with her by their side they'd have drinks flowing their way all night. Mocha took Jaylin's advice and chilled realizing that at midnight it was still early for the club. After a few more drinks Jaylin pulled Mocha out on the dance floor and it seemed as if they were the stars of the night. They moved their bodies to the sound of the hottest hip hop tracks hooked up by the DJ and they heard several whistles.

"Them bitches getting it!" They heard a few females call out.

"Ayye! Get it bitch!" Jaylin said to Mocha as she shook her ass.

Both girls had decided to go with mini dresses. However, Jaylin's was a black tube top and Mocha's was teal with sleeves and a lace cut out on the back. The heels she chose to wear made her ass sit up just right in her dress causing it to shake viciously whenever she twerked. Mocha was enjoying herself so thoroughly she didn't even witness the entourage of twenty niggas enter the club. Her hands were in the air and she had just started to get it to Ciara's voice coming out of the speakers when she felt a hand on the small of her back. She turned around to slap whoever had fucked up her groove but stopped when she realized she was staring into the sexiest pair of hazel eyes she'd ever seen. She caught herself quickly though before the nigga could see her get all googly eyed and shit.

"Excuse you," she said and rolled her eyes rudely.

"Nah excuse you ma," he smiled cockily down at her from his 6'2 build. "You in my city dancing like you ain't got no man so I thought I'd fix that problem."

Mocha had to admit, dude was sexy as shit! Although she usually went for the chocolate guys she had to admit he was one of the sexiest men she'd ever seen in her life. He had to be mixed with something, she could tell by the curls that were neatly on top of his head. When he smiled she could see two deep dimples and a perfect white smile. She gave him a once over and decided that if it weren't for his cocky ass attitude he might have been worth her time. He was dressed in a True Religion fit with a pair of the newest J's out. About one hundred thousand dollars' worth of diamonds rested on his wrist.

"Nah," Mocha said peeping his game. "I think you have me confused with one of these sloppy females in this bitch."

Mocha knew by the thirsty stares the women in the club were giving. The man standing before her must be a hot commodity in Atlanta. She didn't even notice the two goons he had standing behind him as he talked to her. She didn't care though, no matter how big he was he looked like the type who thought he could have whatever he wanted and Mocha refused to be one of those obtainable items. She turned back to Jaylin who had stopped dancing and was looking shocked at Mocha. She couldn't believe she was dissing a boss like the one who stood before her.

"My feet are a little tired," she told Jaylin. "You wanna go take a seat?"

She nodded but before she even answered Mocha was walking past her through the overly crowded dance floor. Mocha added an extra switch in her step just in case eyes were watching all the way to a vacant table.

"Mocha!" Jaylin exclaimed as soon as she caught up. "What the fuck girl? Do you know who that is?"

"Clearly a hustler," Mocha waived her hand in the air. "That nigga looks like he's used to just coming to any club and picking his victim, fuck that."

"Bitch so the fuck what? That's Khiron girl! That nigga is a walking bank, since his daddy got popped a while back he's been on. Running the city like a fuckin' boss since age nineteen," Jaylin said giving Mocha the spill on Khiron while Mocha tried not to trail his every move in the club. "And let me be the first to tell you, I ain't never seen that fine muhfucka approach a bitch at a club."

She emphasized the word "never," to let Mocha know she'd made a big mistake by ignoring Khiron's advances. Mocha rolled her eyes at her.

"Bitch I don't give a fuck, I'm only here for a fuckin' weekend and then back to Detroit I go!" Mocha tried to sound uninterested but in all honesty what she'd just heard sparked her attention.

Mocha studied Khiron from where she sat and whenever they were close to connecting eyes she shifted her gaze. It was going quite well until he tricked her by doing a double take. For ten seconds they stared at each other from across the club through a small window that the mass number of bodies provided.

"You feeling him," Jaylin told her when she stood up to dance with a guy who'd grabbed her hand. "Once in a lifetime chances are only once in a lifetime. Make your move!"

Mocha sighed when her new found friend was whisked away on the dance floor.

"Fuck it," she said under her breath and a flash of Antwan back home came to mind. "That nigga is probably fuckin' some hood rat right now anyway."

Mocha stood up and slowly made her way to where Khiron sat in the VIP section of the club. As soon as she got a little too close for comfort one of his goons stopped her with a hard hand to her chest.

"Aye chill, she's coo people," Khiron said to the man and waived me over to sit on the couch next to him.

"I think we got off on the wrong foot," Mocha flashed her sexiest smile at him.

Might as well go for the dick, she thought to herself as she watched him wet his lips with his tongue. This nigga is sexy as fuck!

"Nah I feel you ma, and I actually respect you more for saying fuck me the first time," he said pouring her a drink.

"I'm only nineteen," Mocha told him truthfully. "I don't drink. But if you have some kush I'll surely blow one with you."

Khiron was shocked to find out her age, especially since she had the body of a grown woman but he was pleased to hear her honesty.

"Aight ma," Khiron chuckled a bit. "Maybe later, but right now let the music fade to the back of our minds and get to know each other a little better first."

They sat in the corner of the club talking for the rest of the time they were at the club. Mocha was so comfortable with him, it felt as if she were talking to someone she'd known her whole life. The conversation between them flowed aimlessly and it came to light that they had many things in common. Before the night was *over they'd blown two blunts and he'd even gotten her to take a shot of tequila. When it was time to leave and everybody was heading to the door Khiron grabbed Mocha by her hand. By talking to her he knew she'd be gone the next day to go home to Detroit and he felt as if he had to spend the night with her. Not even to get her panties, he just wanted to spend some more time with her.*

"Come home with me tonight ma," he told her in sincerity.

"The fuck I look like?" Mocha asked a little offended, even though she'd wanted to jump his bones since she saw him. She still didn't want to come off as an easy hoe. "A fucking one nighter?"

Khiron shook his head.

"Nah ma nothing like that. I just enjoy your company that's all. We ain't gotta do nothing like that if you don't want to," he pulled her close to him so that their lips were barely touching. "Just say yes shorty...please? I'll make sure you get back to the dorms safely in the morning. Just stay the night with me."

Mocha melted in his arms and the look in her eyes gave him his answer. She couldn't say no, because in all honesty she didn't want to. She found Jaylin in the parking lot of the club and told her she'd get a ride back to the room in the morning. Jaylin gave Mocha a knowing look.

"Be careful, niggas like Khiron are only good for one night. I saw y'all getting' friendly over there, don't call yourself falling for a nigga like that. It's never a good thing," Jaylin said.

Mocha nodded her head like she was really listening. The only thing on her mind was the night she had ahead of her with a man that she had just met. Mocha went on to have the night of her life, and ever since was hooked on Khiron.

Mocha snapped back to reality as she whipped her car as fast as she could towards the airport. Her bags were already in her trunk, they'd been packed for days.

"I'm on my way baby," she said smiling at the thought of being reunited with the love of her life.

"Please Khiron!" the voice of a man screamed for mercy but no one could hear him.

Khiron stood over a man who was bound tightly to a chair with a box of matches in his hand. He'd already poured gasoline around the chair and with one match the man's body would go up into flames. The victim in the seat was someone Khiron had to dispose of. He knew too much and was planning to go to the FBI with information about the drug operation Khiron was running in Atlanta. After Khiron's dad got pegged for a little bitch snitching on him to the Italians there was nothing he couldn't stand more. Snitches made the earth stink in his eyes and the world needed to be rid of them if anyone expected to make any money.

"You were going to tesify against me my nigga? Put all my work into the dirt huh?" Khiron laughed at the petrified expression on the man's face. Any hope for mercy was long gone? "Nigga by the time this fire is out there won't be a body to put in the dirt."

"Man I'm sorry! I got a kid and a wife man," the man began to sob like a little bitch and Khiron looked at him disgustedly.

I know this pussy ass nigga ain't start crying? Khiron thought shaking his head. Hell Nah, and this nigga was down with my shit? I'ma have to do a sweep of my own team soon.

"Yea I know you got a shorty, and a little son," Khiron acknowledged the man's family. "And as soon as I'm done here both of them muhfuckas going to have lead in their fuckin skulls! You were going to snitch on me? I'm a fuckin boss, and you? You a bitch, and dogs get put to sleep!"

Without hesitation Khiron lit a match and threw it on the ground by the chair. The man gave a spin tingling scream as he erupted into flames fighting against the ropes that bound him to the chair. There was no hope for him, he had no other choice but to sit there and die. Khiron watched satisfied that he'd finally made his mark. He'd gotten to J Will just before the feds put him into protective custody. Khiron had ears all over the city and once he heard that J Will was planning on singing to the cops. He snatched him up and tortured him in the middle of nowhere, Until he told him that he was in fact planning to testify and putting him away for good. The feds had been hot on Khiron after he caught a body outside of a local strip club. It was a rookie move, but the nigga stepped and Khiron made him fall. The feds couldn't link the body to him because no one would testify and one of his goons disposed of the murder weapon within minutes of the happening. Khiron felt his cell phone vibrate on his hip, he smiled slightly seeing it was from his own shorty.

Hey baby! I'm here and I'm wearing that color you like.

Khiron grinned knowing Mocha was probably laid out butt ass naked in his bed because the color he liked was her mocha skin tone. He'd waited a month to get a taste of that and he wasn't going to let a bitch ass snitch waste anymore of his time.

Handlin some business ma, I'ma be there as soon as I'm done. I love you.

He placed his phone back on his hip after sending his message and spit into the literally screaming fire. He went and got in his black Range Rover that was parked in the grass taking one last look at the fire.

"Burn bitch," he said and drove in the direction towards home where his lady was waiting for him.

♟ CHAPTER 13

Ray walked through the silent halls of his estate towards Sadie's wing. After Coopa sent his goons to his last home he took every precaution to ensure that nothing like that would ever happen again. He had his eighty thousand square foot home built quickly and in secret. His home was unlisted in any phone book or GPS, the only way to get there was to know exactly where it was. As a boy growing up he went on many adventure that took him far from home. The land Ray purchased to build his home was discovered due to one of those adventures. I was surrounded by nothing but trees and a large beautiful pond that Ray also purchased. The home was ducked off and out of the way of mankind but still as a safety precaution he had cameras on the outside of the house and large gates around it. Ray also had two of his hired hands was at the front of the gate every hour of the day. Ray knew that he would be gone often on business and wanted to be certain that Mocha and Sadie would be well taken care of while he was away. Ray had house keepers to help out and keep things orderly around the place. They had their own rooms and free reign of the home, everywhere except their bedrooms and his office. Mocha and Sadie each had their own wing in the house but when they were both home you could always find them together. Currently however

Mocha was gone on a trip to Atlanta and had been gone for a little over a week. He'd checked up on it and found that she had business there and was bringing home big sums of money. He respected her grind and trusted her even more for bringing the money to their business instead of being snake about it.

Ray knocked lightly on Sadie's tall double doors once he arrived.

"Come in!" her voice called on the other side.

He entered a room fit for a queen, and quickly spotted her sitting in her window seat. Sadie's room was like a large suite, kitchen and all. If she never wanted to leave it she didn't have to. When his house was being built Ray had special import and modification requirements. He wanted Sadie to feel like a bag of money whenever she went to bed and woke up. The room was draped in nothing but Versace. Without including the 65 inch TV that hung on her wall, her kind sized bed and other furniture, or the two closets filled with designer clothes and shoes he was standing in a five hundred thousand dollar room.

"Hey," Sadie smiled up at him wearing nothing but a T shirt and a pair of skinny jeans.

Ray knelt and sat down by her feet. He studied her face and couldn't believe how much she'd grown up. Her beauty was breath taking and he was glad that she was focused on making money and not on any niggas. A year before then she was a college student and like his kid sister. Now sitting before him Ray could see the difference. A major difference and Ray knew why. She'd taken a life...a few lives actually. Ray noticed that the innocent blind to the world look was gone from her eyes only to be replaced with a look of hunger and anticipation. Ray couldn't see her as his little cousin anymore. At the age of twenty one she was a grown woman and clearly knew how to handle herself. Sadie flipped her work faster than anyone he'd ever seen. Although he taught her a few things Sadie already knew the game like the back of her hand. Ray was feeling a little guilty. As the new boss of the city all of attention had energy had been on moving product in and out of the city and he hadn't had any time to spend with Sadie. They all had been staying together but if it wasn't about business they barely said two things to each other. Sitting there in front of her he took his time with his words.

"We making money out here fam," Ray said turning to look at Sadie's gorgeous view of the pond. The sun rays made it look blue like the ocean. "The Last Kings...us."

Sadie smiled a small smile.

"The last of a dying breed," she spoke softly turning her head away from the window ever so slightly. Her long silky hair fell in front of her eye.

Ray reached and pushed it behind her ear and nodded. The smile he wore on his face wasn't happy, it was a sad one.

"I never wanted this life for you Say. You were supposed to stay and school. Be a doctor or some shit, not this" he shook his head and leaned back once more. "But the fact remains that you got something that *none* of these niggas got when it comes to this game. You got the heart of a hustler."

Ray stopped as he reflected on what Grandmas Rae used to say to Sadie growing up.

"Sadie, you're Grandma Rae's special baby. Your heart is special. Make this world, don't let it make you."

Sadie's ambition and loyalty to the game was something Ray knew he was going to need. Ray remembered when they were younger and Grandma Rae could only afford to put twenty dollars a month in their pockets. Sadie would take her money to the candy store and spend it all. She sold the candy at school and like a slanger on the corner she tweaked the prices so that the students would still buy but so that she would also make a good profit. Since candy at school was like cocaine to a crack house all the kids flocked to her. Soon it was nothing to flip twenty dollars into three hundred in a matter of days. Ray knew her game was tight when she started bringing shopping bags home that he nor their grandmother bought.

She actually got expelled from the first high school that she attended while staying with Grandma Rae. It turned out that Sadie was the head of an operation at school that sold things, nothing illegal however. Somehow she got her hands on a piece of paper with the schedules of every student and teacher. It also told her when and where a classroom would be vacant. She would have one of her team send out a mass text to an exclusive number of students letting them know when and where to come to shop. Her shop was only open fifteen minutes a day to keep it lowkey. Sadie had moved up from selling candy. She started selling designer clothes she purchased on sale with the money from the original candy operation. She then sold them to all the scandalous bitches and raggedy niggas at school for the low trying to get their stunt on. Sadie had the good shit too. Gucci, True Religion, Dior dresses, Abercrombie & Fitch, etc. You name it and for the right price Sadie got it.

Ray was beyond impressed when he overheard his grandmother and uncle discussing it one night. She single handedly started her own business at school and was bringing in a minimum of five thousand a week. Ray had that in mind the day he handed her that pistol. If she could flip work like that at age sixteen, he could only imagine what she could do with cocaine. The need to make money burned a fire in her eyes and Ray knew that she was a valuable asset to The Last Kings and to himself. Out of all the six businesses she was bringing in the most money, effortlessly. Ray knew at that very moment Sadie was making a one hundred and fifty thousand dollar deal, but she didn't feel as if that was enough money for her to show her face so she did a conference call and had the money wired. Some of their soldiers were going to be making the drop. The way she moved her work was impeccable. Ray was a real nigga so he could admit how crucial losing Sadie would be for his business. He also knew that out of everyone, including Tyler, Sadie was the one he could trust with everything. He knew this because they shared all of the same values and he knew *that* because he instilled them in her.

"I've been so wrapped up into this shit that I haven't even taken the time to ask you how you've been," Ray shook his head disgusted with himself.

"Nah you're good," Sadie reassured him. "We've all been busy, even Mocha! This cartel has to be strong, you never know when a hating ass nigga is going to try and go to war. We have all the time in the world to spend time, right now it's about getting this money the best way we know how."

Ray smiled at Sadie's words and nodded once in respect. Unlike most people Sadie got it. She understood the way of life when cocaine was involved, you got no time off. Unless you cousin ran the whole city. The Last Kings ran Detroit and over the last year the city saw more money than it had in ten years.

"I feel you on that," Ray reached in his pocket and grabbed something out. "But every boss needs a break."

He handed Sadie the contents in his hand and when she saw what they were her face lit up.

"Jamaica?! Oh my God!" Sadie's eyes widened as she looked at the tickets.

"The perfect place to let loose, lay low, and have a good fuckin' time," Ray told her reminiscing on his few trips to Jamaica. "And it will give me a chance to pick ya mind a little."

"When are we going?" Sadie asked rolling her eyes although the effect was thrown off by the big smile on her face.

Ray smiled mischievously and took the tickets back .

"Pack your bags shorty, our flight leaves in the morning."

♟ CHAPTER 14

My bags were packed in less than two hours and I barely got any sleep. I was too ecstatic to be leaving the country. Never in my twenty years of life did I think I would ever get such an opportunity. The fact that Ray was placing it at my feet brought me even more joy. I was a little upset that Mocha wouldn't be joining us but that was cool. I knew she was doing her thing in the A and getting that Last King money. Early the next morning my personal house keeper Maria assisted me with waking up and getting dressed. She was a tiny older woman and she put me in the mind of Grandma Rae. Ray tried to get her to move in with us but she declined insulted. She had owned her house for more than thirty years and wasn't going to give that up. So having Maria was a good thing on my part especially since she treated me with the kindness and love a grandmother would give a granddaughter. After the last bag was placed inside of the Hummer limo parked outside of the house I gave her a big hug knowing it would be three days before I saw her again.

"Maria?" I said into her hair.

"*Si Senora*?" Maria said releasing me holding my hands.

"Do me a favor and don't do any work for the next three days," I smiled big because she and I both knew that wasn't going to happen.

Maria gave a big laugh.

"Senora working is in my blood," she looked lovingly into my eyes. "*You* do me a favor and have a good time ok?"

I nodded and with one last hug I let the driver open my door and I climbed in the limo across from Ray. The limo was decked the fuck out with a TV and a mini bar. I was thinking *"OK!! I'm feeling this!"* Even though I drove an all black Range Rover, I was still loving the luxury.

"You ready?" Ray asked cheesing and rubbing his fingers on his goatee.

"I'm ready," I smiled at him feeling the butterflies in my stomach. "I've never been on a plane before."

"Well there's a first time for everything right?" He asked me and motioned for the driver to pull off.

I turned to look out the tinted window at Maria once more. I knew she couldn't see me but she waived never the less as the limo pulled off, I smiled and leaned back in my seat knowing that ahead of me lies a beautiful paradise.

"I gotta go holla at Tyler before we hit the airport," Ray told me.

"Cutting it close don't you think?" I asked weary we could potentially miss our flight.

"We'll be coo," he turned to the right slightly and yelled to get the drivers attention. "Pierre! Make a stop at Amore!"

I watched Pierre, a little African man, tip his hat acknowledging Ray's words. He drove us through the woods and finally we reached a highway. We had two hours before our flight left and we had to be there an hour before. Pierre got us to Amore in less than fifteen minutes, that nigga was flooring the gas to get us there in a timely manner.

I stared at the outside of the building I saw daily and felt a twinge of pride. I ran it day in and day out. Unknown to any federal agency Amore saw a minimum of two-hundred thousand dollars daily. As the heart of The Last Kings I had to make sure business was conducted regularly. Ray told me that Tyler would be overseeing the business while we were away, but I was a little worried just because no one knew how to run it better than me. I knew the clients like the back of my hand, I guess all of those research papers in college I did had some type of purpose in my life after all. I dug so deep into those muhfucka's files I knew what hand they wiped their asses with and why. No one was going to get over on me or shut my shit down. The women I had working the club below were superb, no blemishes could be found on their bodies. They all had attributes to make the eyes of any man pop and were all nationalities. I didn't consider myself a pimp or a madam or whatever the fuck they were called now a days. The women who worked for me were women who had nothing and nobody to depend on *but* us. They were orphans...rejects. Like me, but not like me at all. I purchased a nice house for them all to live in and I paid them well. So well that none of them would ever even think to be the birdie to chirp to any fed ass nigga. There was only one rule...One way in, no way out. Once you were down with The Last Kings you got branded for life. The pyramid on their bodies showed their alliance to us and if they ever wanted to stop working in the club at Amore then they could, but they would have to put in work in another part of the operation. If they wanted *out* then my .48 would see to it that that happened.

"I'm coming in," I told Ray as Pierre opened our door. I needed to see first-hand my shit was going to be taken care of.

Ray smirked and shook his head.

"Everything is going to be straight Say," he knew exactly why I wanted to go in.

"Yea whatever, I need to see this shit for myself," I said exiting the limo before he could.

"We'll be right back Pierre," Ray said and walked quickly after me.

I entered the restaurant and once we were spotted we received an array of love.

"Ms. Sadie! How are you today?"

"You look fabulous!"

"Ray, my man! Looking like a sack of money, but what's new?"

We smiled and greeted everyone from servers to customers. Although it was an Italian restaurant with mostly Italian customers our faces had become implanted into the foundation of the place. Ray's business with the Italians was proving to be the best partnership and I truly felt like I was surrounded by family. We walked to the secret entrance of the club and found Tyler in the money room of course. He was looking fresh as usual in Ralph Lauren from head to his toes. The fade on his curly head was fresh and he gave me a knowing look once he saw me.

"I should've known yo ass wasn't going to leave without stopping by," Tyler said smirking at me smugly as he finished rolling a joint.

I gave Tyler a sideways glance and made my way past him to look at the counts so far but before I could get to them he stepped in front of me. His Ralph Lauren cologne invaded my nostrils and I stopped in my tracks although I was not able to stop the butterflies from fluttering in my gut.

"Everything is coo ma, don't trip," Tyler said seriously.

"Move out of my way Tyler," I said trying to sound rude.

"Put them fuckin' claws away Say," Ray said chuckling. "My man is only doing what I asked. You on vacation shortly, you been working non stop since you been on. Tyler is going to hold down the spot for you starting now."

"But—" I was cut off by Ray's hand being held up and I knew it would be futile to argue instead I rolled my eyes in defeat.

"So what's real my nigga?" Ray asked Tyler.

"We got a business proposal," Tyler said simply and my interest peaked.

Ray was used to hearing those words so his demeanor didn't change. He was on an up rise and a handful of there were a handful of niggas trying to get put on. Ray turned all of them away, you had to be chosen to be down with his operation. I wondered at times if I wasn't family if he would have taken such a leap of faith with me and Mocha.

"Alright, so what's up?"

"I ain't really wanna tell you right now since you about to be on a trip and shit," Tyler shrugged and I knew he could really give two fucks about our trip money came first. "Dude from Atlanta hit me up, says he's looking for some big work. I told him we got it, but if it ain't legit business we can't fuck with em'. Also told em' he has to go through the big man first. You."

I studied Ray's face. From the sounds of it someone was looking at Ray to be their connect. That would be a first. Ray mainly sold to clients and those residing in his area. When it came to getting his business in other cities Ray did it himself and he headed those operations too.

"Who is it?" Ray asked.

"The nigga's name is Khiron, he's hot in the A I guess," Tyler told him.

"Yea I heard of that nigga. His pops used to push some heavy work back in the day. He was on some Coopa shit though, and ended the same way," Ray nodded his head. "If that nigga is anything like his pops I won't fuck with it."

Tyler nodded his head agreeing.

"I did some research on the little nigga though bro," Tyler sat down and leaned back in his chair. "He's bringing in mad work in the A. Word on the street is that his connect just got bumped up. Nigga is looking at life with no chance of ever seeing the outside world again."

Ray's dreads shook slightly as he cocked his head interested.

"So the nigga is thirsty, I feel him. How much he throwing?"

Tyler sparked his joint and took a long draw from it.

"Here's the fuckin' kicker bro," Tyler sat forward rubbing his light hand across his face. "He wants to talk business. Face to face, he wants to do some big business with us. I guess he heard what The Last Kings is doing in the dope game and wants a slice of this pie. Only thing is the kind of pie and how big his slice is, is up to you."

"Aight, and when does he want to conduct his business?" Ray asked.

I looked at Tyler as he fixed his mouth to speak knowing what he was about to say before the word was out.

"Tomorrow," Tyler said grinning sheepishly.

I rolled my eyes and looked at Ray. My visions of paradise faded away, business always came first. I knew that but I couldn't lie and say I wasn't a slight bit disappointed. I tried to remove the disappointment from my face but Ray still saw it.

"Aight," Ray said running his fingers through his dreads the way he did when he was deep in thought. "I'ma hold down shit here, Tyler you're going to go in my place to Jamaica fam, it's only three days."

Both Tyler and I looked at him and then at each other. What Ray was informing us was that he wanted Tyler to accompany me overseas, alone. The look in Tyler's eyes said he didn't think it was a good idea and the butterflies in my stomach agreed.

"Are you sure fam? You might need me here," Tyler asked still looking at me.

"For what?" Ray asked picking up a stack of hundreds and holding it up for us to see. "The flow of this shit never stops. Go, Pierre is waiting, he has the plane tickets."

I broke eye contact with Tyler and smiled at Ray.

"Thanks fam, just don't burn down this bitch down while I'm gone," I whispered into his ear giving him a hug.

"Watch after her, and make sure she has the best time possible. You feel me?" Ray said with one good squeeze and then let me go.

Tyler stood up and shook Ray's hand.

"You know it," Tyler said. "Well lets go then shorty. We don't want to miss *our* flight now do we?"

I cut my eyes at him and gave Ray one last farewell before leading Tyler to the limo.

"I was starting to think you weren't coming back," Pierre said opening my door.

"No I'm definitely going, but there has been a slight change in plans," I said nodding my head backwards to Tyler. "Ray's staying but this nigga is coming."

"This nigga?" Tyler asked in his deep voice laughing. "What's up Pierre, just try and get us to the airport in one piece."

"Will do," Pierre smiled at the two of us and winked at me.

I didn't know what that was all about but it was almost like he knew something I didn't. He shut the door behind us and once he climbed in himself we were on our way. Tyler sat across from me and I couldn't help but notice how handsome he was. His mother was a white woman and his daddy was black as night. The mixture of the two gave him a nice smooth light brown skin tone. His facial hair was perfectly trimmed and lined along his powerful jawbone structure. His eyes were hazel and cold as ice, but that came with the job. His body structure was similar to Ray's, big, muscled, and intimidating. I tried not to stare but it was like I was seeing him for the first time in years and as my gaze traveled down to the one thing that remained hidden his voice interrupted my almost naughty thoughts.

"Excited?" Tyler asked me showing his perfect pearly whites.

"A little bit," I smiled at him wondering if he'd been watching me study him that whole time.

"Shot?" Tyler went into the bar and got out a bottle of Hennessey and two shot glasses. "Real niggas drink dark liquor."

"Don't mind if I do," when I reached to grab the tiny glass Tyler had poured the liquor into our hands brushed slightly together and I felt a tingly feeling in the pit of my stomach.

It was a feeling that I'd been fighting off for years. I had a secret. If Ray knew that secret he may not have let me go thousands of miles away with Tyler. Tyler was like a big cousin to me and more so he was Ray's right hand man from the jump so any attraction I felt for him had to be ended. When I was in my senior year of high school I tried to test the waters and see how far I could get before having to resurface. I remembered that night like it was yesterday, it was the reason being alone with Tyler was more than a little awkward. Tyler used to stay the night at Grandma Rae's house all the time and my budding crush for him had turned into a burning desire to feel him inside of me. The feelings I had for him were so real, or they seemed like it. After all of the sexual trauma I'd gone through. It was hard giving myself away to just anyone. I hated sex, after Nino I had only slept with two other guys and I regretted both times. But for some reason I had it in my mind that I had to have Tyler.

At that age all the girls were on Tyler and Ray, but I had already claimed Tyler as mine. I would sometimes catch him staring curiously at me...not in the way a guy looked at his best friend's kid cousin. In his eyes there was a longing. We used to kick it all the time. He would pick me up from school and we would just ride and talk about nothing, but everything. He told me that I was smart and could be anything I wanted to be in life and I remember wanting to tell him all I wanted to be was his girl. Even though I knew he would just turn my young ass away with all the grown pussy being thrown his way. While he was asleep in Ray's room one night, Ray was gone I don't remember why he was I just remember he wasn't there. I snuck in the room after deciding that it was time for me to make my move. I blinked and in one quick moment my eyes shut and I reminisced on how things played that night.

He was sleeping soundly when I entered the room with nothing but my bathrobe hiding my eighteen year old body. I turned on some sensual R&B music and dimmed the lights to set the mood. As I stared before me I licked my lips just at the thought of climbing on top of Tyler. The Tyler, all the girls in my class wanted a piece of that and I was going to be the one to get it. I knew he was feeling me just by how he looked at me, I knew I'd finally grown into my body and now was the time to put it to work. Ray had a king sized bed and I softly mounted it, barely making it move as I crawled like a lioness toward her prey. Tyler slept shirtless and on his back which made it easier to straddle him. I let the music take its toll on my mindset and slowly let my robe drop exposing my perky breasts. I was excited for Tyler to see and take me all for himself but still I decided to move slowly. I lowered my body and kissed his soft lips, just a peck. But that was all that was needed to stir him. I then let my tongue travel to his neck and to his exposed chest.

"Mmm," he moaned softly still not yet all the way awake

"You like that baby?" I whispered seductively.

When he nodded his head I leaned back in and began to kiss him passionately and he returned it. I felt his warm hands explore every depth of my body and my treasure began to drip with juices. His hands squeezed my ass and pinched my nipples sensually, but his eyes still did not open once. I let my hand slide down towards his briefs and massage his manhood. Feeling it in my hand made me more eager to let it slide inside of me. His dick was huge and lived up to any stories told about him. Actually I didn't think the stories did him justice. Lowering my pelvis I began to grind slowly to the slow beat of the song that was playing.

"Oooh shit," Tyler breathed.

"Can I have it?" I whispered into his ear.

"Do you want it?" Tyler asked sticking his fingers deep inside my treasure.

I bit my lip and squeezed my walls tightly around his finger.

"Yes," I barely breathed. I couldn't believe it was about to happen and I circled my hips on his fingers as they thrust in and out of me.

"Oh fuck this shit is wet ma," he whispered into the air eyes still shut.

Tyler gripped my waist and with one swift move threw me on the bed with him on top of me. His strength turned me on and my hands clawed at his body. Our lips met again and I somehow ripped his briefs off more than ready to be one with him. Just as he was about to enter me, his face inches from mine his eyes opened and I was staring into the most beautiful pair of hazel eyes I'd seen in my life.

"Say?" He said and the horror in his voice broke my heart. "What the fuck do you think you're doing shorty?"

He jumped up and stared at me with disgust in his eyes.

"Calm down!" I tried to hush him not wanting to wake Grandma Rae. I wrapped the cover around my nude body trying to hide myself.

Tyler took a deep breath and tried to calm himself.

"What were you thinking Say?" Tyler calmed his voice down. "What if someone would have come in and saw you trying to...to —"

"I'm sorry," I said in a meek voice hanging my head. "I just thought you wanted me...like I want you."

Tyler sighed and ran his hands over his curly fade.

"Look Say, you're like my lil cousin. I don't think about you like that," Tyler said in a softer tone probably

not wanting to hurt my feelings more than he already had.

"You wanted me a second ago," I whispered.

"A second ago my eyes were closed," He said forcefully. "This is my fault shorty, I should have never let you catch me slipping."

I just nodded my head and grabbed my robe.

"Let's just act like this never happened aight?"

I didn't say a word, just got up and ran out of the room. Pretend was right, Tyler had broken my heart. I would pretend that I never had feelings for him at all.

My eyes opened and I smiled at Tyler as he sat grown and suave before me holding up his glass.

"Cheers," he said.

"Cheers," I smiled and clanked his glass with mine.

This is going to be an interesting three days, I thought with a smirk and welcomed the burning sensation as I emptied my glass.

♟ CHAPTER 15

Mocha quietly climbed out of Khiron's king sized bed in her nighty not wanting to wake him. It was her last morning with him and she wanted to surprise him with breakfast in bed. She tip toed her way through Khiron's large house to his over-sized kitchen and went to work. Chicken and waffles, breakfast fit for a king! That's what he was, her king. Mocha hadn't meant to fall in love with Khiron, but after all of the trips to Atlanta and all the time they'd spent together it was hard not to. She felt bad for keeping secrets from him and even more so her team, but she felt that she was entitled to a personal life. A life no one but she could control. She also felt that it was vital to keep her affiliation with The Last Kings secret. Although he was a hustler in Atlanta. He was pulling in heavy weight in his own city. His operation wasn't moving nearly as much work as The Last Kings and Mocha felt that would put a huge dent in their relationship. As far as Khiron knew she was still a student working part time at a local bank. Who said a good relationship couldn't be built on a lie? Mocha also knew Khiron's temper, she'd been present for enough killings and kidnappings. Khiron was the type of nigga who just didn't give a fuck. Whereas Ray's heart was cold, Khiron simply didn't have one; only with Mocha. She didn't know how he would take it if he found out his girl saw more money in one day then he did in two months. She knew Atlanta was a hard market, so she had been giving them work at a lower price. She wasn't anyone's connect, but the product she provided the city kept its drug ring afloat. Mocha also knew if Khiron found that out he would flip the script.

"*Baabbyy*," Mocha purred into Khiron's ear once his breakfast was made and sat on a small table tray before him.

"Mmm," Khiron stirred before finally opening his eyes. Once he saw the food in front of him a big smile crossed his fame. "Damn ma, you the fuckin' best!"

Mocha returned his smile and handed him his eating utensils.

"Eat up!" She said.

And that he did. The air was filled with smacking and chewing. In less than ten minutes the plate was completely clean. Mocha stared at the plate shocked wondering if the nigga had been starving.

"Damn," Mocha said cutting her eyes seductively at him. "With all that eating you did last night I didn't think you'd be that hungry."

Khiron grinned and pushed the tray to the floor causing the dishes to make a large clanking noise.

"Girl you know I can never get enough of you, a nigga is always hungry!" He pulled her on top of him and they shared a passionate kiss before Mocha pulled away.

"I have to hop in the shower babe, you know my plane leaves in three hours!" Mocha said.

Khiron looked at the clock and saw t read ten o clock and remembered that her flight took off at one o clock. He knew how Mocha was. Early was on time. He smiled at her and squeezed her bottom for good measure.

"Aight ma, it's coo. Leave your man laying here with a hard dick. I see how it is," Khiron told her playfully.

Mocha rolled her eyes at him and kissed him one last time.

"Boy, your dick is always hard, what's new?" She laughed at him and got up from the bed. "You can join me if you'd like," she winked at him.

"Nah, I'm good right here," Khiron wasn't yet ready to get out of bed.

"Suit yourself," Mocha shrugged her shoulders and disappeared inside of the bathroom in the bedroom.

Once she was out of sight Khiron sighed and shook his head. He didn't know what he was doing anymore. Mocha was meant to be only a fling, but here it was coming up on a year and the bitch was still in and out of his crib. She was honestly the only bitch that had ever even seen the inside of his home. He hadn't meant to develop such strong feeling for the girl, but he couldn't help it. She was smart, independent and sassy just like he liked them. Not to mention her body put Beyonce's to shame. But Khiron also knew love in the dope game got you killed, and he wasn't ready to die. Especially not over pussy. That's how his pops went out and he for damn sure wasn't going to follow in his footsteps. His dad was one of the greatest dopeman to ever grace the streets of Atlanta. That nigga could push work in his sleep. But for some reason he started using the product he was distributing on the streets and in the end was caught slipping; deaded in his own home. It was all bad for Khiron when he found that out. He was nineteen and at the age where he would have inherited all of his father's empire. Instead all he got was a box of his father's old videos that he accidently left with Khiron's mother, his father's old machete, and a few pieces of jewelry. Khiron had to fight for his rightful place at the top and put many bodies under.

Once his pops was dead Atlanta went crazy. Everybody was trying to be the next kingpin even though there could only be one. Eventually Khiron claimed his right to fame by killing any nigga in his way. Khiron watched the videos his father left behind several times, and each time got knots in his stomach. The videos clearly showed the face of the one who betrayed his father...someone close to him. Too close. Khiron swore on his grave that he would avenge his death once he located them but in the meantime he was in a sticky situation when it came to his cartel. Shit was going smooth for him. His business was expanding but after a huge drug bust his connect wound up in prison. He got life without a chance of parole. Now Khiron was stuck with serving a city with no fucking connect. No connect meant no money. No connect mean no cartel and he couldn't have that. Once his well ran dry that would be the end of the road for him, but he wasn't with that. He wasn't tripping too hard though knew off tops where he could find a connect. Detroit. Mocha's home. He wanted to ask her if she knew anything about The Last Kings even though he knew she couldn't. The operation was too smooth and lowkey. He knew they were getting millions of dollars. The stories he heard about them sound-

ed like myths and urban legends but he knew they exist-
ed and it wouldn't be hard for him to get a number.
When Coopa was still running shit in the city they'd
crossed paths a few times to conduct business and every
time Khiron remembered a nigga by the name of Ray
being there. When he first met with them he made the
mistake of shaking Ray's hand first mistaking him for
Coopa. He just had that aura about him. That nigga had
a presence that could make any nigga bow. Not cocky,
just confident and when Khiron sent a few of his soldiers to scope out Detroit he found that Ray was in fact
the new boss of the city. All he needed to do was get in
contact with him and get the product he needed to push
in his city. There was also another plan in the works;
Detroit was a great market for business. Khiron wanted
it. He didn't mention to Mocha that he would be catching a flight to Detroit a little after hers because he didn't
want her all in his business or checking for him once he
touched down. So he just kept that little piece of info to
himself and if he ran into her in the city he would just
blow her off. There were many more where she came
from.

"Ok, I'm ready to head to the airport!" Mocha said
cheerfully as she emerged through the bathroom door, a
trail of steam followed her.

"Aight shorty, let me throw on some shit and we
can go," Khiron said snapping out of his thoughts.

It's going to be hard to let all that go though, he
thought as he eyed her in a white Louis Vuitton mini
dress that clung to all of her curves and her red pumps.

He shook his head one time and then proceeded to get dressed trying not to let her see his already packed suit cases in the closet.

♟ ♟ ♟

Once Mocha was through the terminal her tiny vacation was swiftly over with one phone call.

"Hello?" She asked into the phone recognizing Devynn's number.

"You back?" Devynn cut right to the chase.

"Just touched down actually," Mocha told her throwing her suit case to the driver of the Mercedes waiting for her in front of the airport.

"Coo, I need you to meet me at Lace tomorrow at nine o-clock sharp," Devynn told her.

"Any particular reason why?" Mocha asked leaning back into the cold leather inside of the luxury vehicle.

"Well if your ass didn't feel the need to go to Atlanta as much as you change thongs. You would know that some little niggas came into the salon this morning trying to rob it and shit," she didn't even try and disguise the annoyance in her voice.

"You coo?" Mocha asked knowing that the salon was all her.

"The question is are them niggas coo and the answer to that is hell Nah," Devynn began telling her the story and Mocha was all ears. "It was early so I was the only one there of course. When I went to the back room to do some counts I heard the window crash. It had to be at least six niggas all strapped. I got three of em' but real shit if Amann hadn't decided to stop by unexpectedly I wouldn't be alive to be talking to yo ass."

"Damn," Mocha said genuinely concerned. "I'm glad you're cool, what Ray say?"

"We think the shit was premeditated. They had to have been watching the spot close for a minute to learn it's schedule and today was a drop off day. One hundred stacks alone were in the back room and they would have had it all if they would have popped me."

"So what's going on a Lace tonight?"

"Bitch we on the phone, just be there aight?" Devynn said insinuating that the phone could be tapped.

"Aight, where's Sadie?" Mocha rolled her eyes at Devynn's quaintness. She never had really liked her, but she dealt with her just because of the business. "Is she going to be there too?"

"You don't know?" Devynn chuckled.

Mocha was confused at what was so funny but tried to keep a steady voice.

"Know what?"

"Girl Sadie ain't here, she probably chilling on the beach somewhere topless and shit. Her and Tyler both actually."

"Hold up," Mocha tried to make sense of her words. "What are you saying?"

"She in Jamaica girl, for a week. She actually just left yesterday with Tyler," Devynn once again didn't try to hide the smugness in her voice.

Mocha although very shocked didn't want to give Devynn the satisfaction.

"Awh ok, that's what's up," she said like she didn't care. But in reality a million and one thoughts were going through her mind.

Why the fuck was Sadie in Jamaica? With Tyler especially? And why the fuck didn't she tell me she was going?

"I'll be there," Mocha said and ended the call.

Sadie kept telling her to chill when it came to Devynn, but Mocha just didn't like her. She knew to be in good with Ray you couldn't be on any snake shit but there was something about her attitude that she didn't like. Sadie often said it was because they were so alike in many ways. Mocha didn't want to admit it, but of course Sadie was right. The two of them were both head strong which made them hard headed. Once stuck in their own way it was impossible making them see reason. Devynn was just cocky and Mocha didn't like that shit. Mocha gave the driver the directions of her destination and she sat back sipping on her chardonnay thinking about what Sadie was up to.

♟ ♟ ♟

"This is beautiful!" I exclaimed leaning over the balcony from my room in the penthouse suite Tyler and I shared. "I can't believe I'm here!"

From my balcony I had the perfect view of the beach. Although we had just returned from the sand and the joys of being swamped by the huge waves I couldn't get over the scenery. I stood there with my towel wrapped around my waist and wet hair loosely hanging over my shoulders. I was sad that Ray wasn't there to embark on my first trip out of the country but I was happy that he chose Tyler to accompany me. We had so much fun at the beach. I never knew that Tyler had such a soft fun loving side, but he was right beside me splashing in the water. He even dunked me a few times, hence my hair being as fucked up as it was. We made a sand castle and he said that it was The Last Kings mark on Jamaica. When I first emerged in my string bikini Tyler's eyes traveled my body for a brief second but that was the only awkward moment in the whole day. He never advanced on me as we ran around like teenagers and I felt at peace. No killing, no guns, no drugs. I forgot what it felt like to just chill out and relax. At home I was always on edge, driving around in bullet proof vehicles and traveling with ten goons at a time. I felt at ease and as long as Tyler was beside me; I felt safe. I was feeling a little sad for not telling Mocha where I was but she was in Atlanta handling business, I didn't want to interrupt anything. She would understand.

"This is my third time being here," Tyler said coming up from behind. "Each time I come I expect it to be less beautiful than before."

"And?" I said smiling up at him.

"It's always as beautiful as before," he smiled back down at me.

I stood there and took in the man before me. He must have hopped in the shower as soon as we hit the door. My nostrils inhaled his Burberry cologne and my eyes took in the white wife beater that hugged his muscular upper body in the sexiest way and the camouflage cargo shorts he wore. On his feet he had a pair of all white Retro Jordan 4's and although a simple fit, I was feeling his fresh. I was supposed to be getting ready too, since we were going to head out to dinner. But I'd gotten distracted by the view. The next words out of my mouth were words I could have kicked myself for but I couldn't stop them from escaping my lips.

"Those bitches must have been something special if you're flying them to Jamaica," I could hear the jealousy dripping from my voice.

Tyler gave a whole hearted laugh and shook his head.

"Nah ma, you got it all wrong," Tyler crossed his arms and turned around so that his back leaned on the balcony.

Fuck it, I thought. I'd already said it might as well go with the flow.

"Oh do I now?" I asked.

"Yea, you do."

"Enlighten me then," I told him.

Tyler looked at me and chuckled shaking his head.

"Aight ma, if you insist. You sounded a little jealous, but I'll peep you on some shit if you can handle it," he smirked at me.

I rolled my eyes at his comment.

"Fuck you Ty, now talk," I wrapped my towel more tightly around my waist.

"Aight ma it's like this, I'm a fuckin' boss. If I feel like taking a trip I'ma buy a fucking ticket. I'm never pressed for pussy but if I have a bitch with me at the time I make my decision then she's going be on that plane with me. If I plan on going on any trip it's either going to be business or pleasure. If it's pleasure I'ma fuck em', pluck em', and when we get back I'm done with that bitch," he told me bluntly.

"I thought you said I had it wrong as in you didn't bring bitches with you," I said smugly trying not to get mad. I mean, I didn't have a reason to be mad. He wasn't my nigga nor would he ever be.

"No I said you had it all wrong 'cause you said they were special," Tyler said matter of factly smirking at me. "And in that sense you had it all wrong."

"Whatever Tyler," I couldn't keep the smile from coming. "One question though."

"What up shorty?"

"What would you classify this as? Business or pleasure?" I knew I was pushing it but I threw him a sexy smile anyway and switched my way to the bathroom inside of my bedroom. Before the door shut I caught one last glimpse of him on the balcony, watching me and biting his lip.

When I was finished cleansing every crevice of my body from sand; I lotioned my body making it silky smooth and decided to wear a coral colored maxi dress. It wasn't too tight and left a few things to the imagination. The top was tubed and it stopped a few inches above my ankles. I chose a pair of nude colored gladiator sandals and accessorized accordingly. I made the choice to match him with my fragrance and once I pinned my still wet curly hair atop of my head in a messy white girl type bun. I walked down the stairs of the suite to see Tyler waiting at the door for me. The smile that spread on his face was priceless.

"You look beautiful," he told me.

"I know," I showed him all of my teeth and walked through the door he held open for me. "Thanks though."

Tyler shook his head at my cockiness.

"I have reservations at this nice spot. It has the best view of the city and it's close enough to walk." he said as he trailed alongside me.

"You took those hoes there?" I asked bumping my hip on his playfully as we made our way through crowds of people.

"You know," Tyler said chuckling, "you need to really get that jealousy shit out cha system ma. The shits not a good look, especially for a boss-ette."

"I'm not jealous!" I snapped. "I just don't wanna go anywhere you shared memories with your bitches."

On the strip Tyler stopped abruptly and grabbed me softly by my shoulders.

"Sadie, chill out. We're here to have a good time and enjoy ourselves. Stop tripping you know I wouldn't disrespect you like that. This is a spot that I actually have only come to by myself, and now I'm sharing it with you. Is that coo?"

I stared up into Tyler's eyes and saw the sincerity in them. Why he felt the need to explain was above my head but I had peace of mind knowing he hadn't been up in the spot with some chicken head. I nodded my "ok," and linked arms with him.

"I've been meaning to ask you something," I told him as we walked through the loud groups of natives and tourists.

The sun was going down and it gave our surroundings a beautiful glow. I never wanted to leave, but I knew this break from business was only temporary. But

I still was curious about the reason why Ray stayed behind. I wanted some info on the person he was meeting but I was waiting for the right moment to ask. Although for the most part I knew everything that was going on in the operation there were some things Ray and Tyler left from the rest of us.

"This way," Tyler said rounding a corner with me in tow. "What's up shorty?"

Just as I was about to answer his question a group of young Jamaicans, all with thick long dreads, approached us on the strip.

"Ay mon!" One of them said with a thick accent. "You smell like money. We dance for you, mon! And we get some?"

I looked at the five young kids and was curious as to what they could do. I'd seen many strange talents on the strip and this one looked like it would be at least semi-normal. One of them had a stereo and he set it down to prepare the act's song.

"What's your name?" Tyler asked in his deep intimidating voice.

"Blaze," the kid said matter of factly and something told me his mother didn't give him that name.

"A'ight let's see what you can do," Tyler told him nodding. "But waste my time and I'll have all you little muhfuckas regretting the shit."

The boys looked at each other somewhat nervous, an actual challenge had been placed on the table and if they didn't beat it there was no telling what the fuck Tyler would do. I folded my arms and stepped back to watch. As they got into their formation to start their performance I felt a crowd slowly forming around us. The beat dropped and once it did they took off. I couldn't keep the smile off of my face as I watched them break dance, it gave me a rush! They were so good they should have been on that show America's Best Dance Crew; these little Jamaican niggas could get it! I grabbed on to Tyler's arm and squealed in joy as they did one final set of flips and ended the show. They of course got a round of applause and Tyler himself even had a grin on his face.

"So what's up mon?" Blaze asked out of breath.

Tyler stared them down for a moment, giving them each eye contact, before he reached in his pocket and peeled five hundred American dollars from a crisp stack of Ben Franks. He gave each of them one and after seeing their eyes grow large he grabbed my hand. Without another word to them we began our journey to the restaurant once more. Seeing all that money in his hands reminded me of the question that I was meaning to ask him.

"So what's up Say?" Tyler asked clearly thinking about the question as well.

"That nigga trying to do business with us—"

"Khiron?" Tyler asked.

"You said he's hot in the A right?" I asked him as we walked.

"Yea something like that. The little nigga is on the come up."

"Why haven't I ever heard of him then? I know every hustler in every city. Why am I missing him?" I asked.

When Ray left me in charge of Amore I did my research. Just in case a war started between us and whoever I wanted to have every city on lock. I needed to know who the fuck was selling to who, who was beefing, and what niggas were plotting. After a few snitching ass niggas gave me all the info I needed on the major drug cartels in the big cities I found that there was no one fuckin' with The Last Kings. The only one cutting close was Legacy in Miami but that nigga wasn't stupid enough to test a nigga of Ray's caliber. See Ray not only had The Last Kings but he had the Italians on his side too, and nobody wanted to fuck with the Italian mafia.

"That nigga been low," Tyler began to explain. "A while back his daddy got murked by the Italians. Nigga had a bad gambling problem, even started tasting his own candy." Tyler shook his head. "After he died though the empire Khiron should have inherited rightfully was dispersed to the greedy hands of Atlanta. The nigga had to practically claw his way from the bottom back to the top which is why when he hit me up on business I figured it was best for Ray to handle the situation."

"Why?" I asked swerving to miss a drunken couple laughing and dancing along the sidewalk.

"Because that means the nigga is hungry," Tyler said, his tone insinuating that I should already know that info. "A hungry nigga can be a good thing because that means he's ready to put in work. But a hungry nigga can also be the worst type of nigga. A hungry nigga can turn snake in a matter of seconds and that nigga Ray can smell a snake from a mile away."

I nodded agreeing with Tyler's judgment on having Ray handle the situation. If the nigga was on snake shit I knew he would never make it back to Atlanta…in one piece anyway.

"We're here," Tyler said bringing us to a stop in front of a small restaurant with all glass windows. I was shocked because I definitely wouldn't have pegged Tyler as the type to enjoy such a place. He must have seen the expression on my face because he smiled. "I'm not too fond of these windows and shit, but the food is enough to keep a nigga coming back! Come on."

I followed him inside and the restaurant was genuinely beautiful. I had never seen anything like it back in the states. It was jungle themed with wild colorful plants hanging and it even had a large fountain in the middle shaped like a waterfall. We were quickly welcomed by a swarm of gorgeous women all looking hungrily at Tyler.

"I see another reason why you come back too," I said under my breath and he seemed not to have heard me. We were seated at a low table by a half dressed woman.

"May I take your order?" she asked Tyler in very good English and completely ignored me.

I couldn't deny it, she was gorgeous, but I knew she for damn sure didn't look better than me. Her hair was short and her mouth was large. She was shapely, but not proportioned well.

"What you want to drink ma?" Tyler asked me and I saw her roll he eyes on the sneak.

"Order me whatever," I told him smiling flirtatiously to piss her off even more. "I know you got me."

Tyler ordered us some food ignoring the attitude the woman had suddenly started giving.

"Will that be all?" She asked sarcastically rolling her eyes openly at me.

"Nah shorty but while you back there get us a new server," Ray told her calmly. "You don't even know me and you pressed for a dick that would never even entertain that big ass duck mouth of yours. Since you're being rude to my guest, the rest of the time I'm here I don't want to see your fucking face aight?"

Tyler stared so coldly at her I swear her chocolate face turned purple before she turned on her heels and basically ran back to the kitchen.

"You better have checked that bitch," I told him hiding my smile. "Those eyes were about to get snatched out of her fuckin' head!"

"You know I got you ma, like you said," he said staring into my eyes.

I bit my lip and had to look away. The way his eyes lingered on mine made me feel something in my stomach that hadn't been felt in years. The last person to make me feel that way was of course the person sitting across from me. There was something about Tyler that I couldn't shake, it had always been like that, I'd just gotten used to ignoring the feeling. But now being alone with him it was proving difficult to not mix business and pleasure in my mind.

"Look at me," Tyler told me.

"I can't," I said truthfully.

"Why not?" Tyler asked.

I sighed. Our vacation was only a week and I would need a lifetime to decipher my emotions. Being around Tyler that short time was making me feel all sorts of feelings for him that I knew I shouldn't have been feeling.

"I just can't," I told him shaking my head looking at everything in the restaurant but him.

Without warning Tyler reached across the table and cupped my chin gently in his hand forcing me to look at him.

"Don't ever be afraid to look at me ma, no matter what," he told me in a soft but stern manner

"But I am afraid," I told him honestly.

"You weren't afraid back at home," Tyler pointed out.

"Home is different. I know what's real when I'm there, I'm protected. But here...it's like I'm living out my fantasies. My dreams."

Tyler stared at me and for a brief second the coldness that lived there disappeared, only to be replaced with a look of longing.

"You remember that night?" He asked in a low voice releasing my chin.

Of course I remembered that night. Because I'd spent the majority of my time the past few years trying to erase it from my memory, I didn't say that though.

"I think about that shit all the time," he kept going and I knew I didn't want to hear what he had to say but my ears were fixated on his words anyway. "I used to tell myself that I didn't know it was you, before I realized that it was. But something in me knew it was. I watched you grow up...you were like Ray's kid sister so I just kind of adopted you as such too. But there was always something different about you and I felt wrong for having those feelings for you. My eyes had traveled your body enough to know how it felt. And when my hands finally did touch…it was like heaven ma. I wanted you so bad. Just like now, I mean look at you. You're beautiful and you have the mindset of greatness. Any man would be lucky to have you on his arm. But I knew then just like I know now that it would never work. I can't be that man. This is business and we can't let our personal feelings jeopardize what we have going. In this world love is a weakness, and that's something I'm not willing to risk. You know it would never work—"

Before he could finish his statement I'd had enough. I wasn't going to sit there as he basically rejected me again. And this time I hadn't even thrown myself at him. It felt as if my heart was being ripped out of my chest and I couldn't handle it. Besides Ray, Tyler was the only other man I'd ever been close to so his words cut me deep. I pushed away from the table and ran out of the restaurant not caring that I bumped into a man carrying two trays of food and caused him to drop everything in his hands.

"Sadie!" I heard Tyler call behind me but I ignored him.

I just wanted to get back to the safeness of my room inside of the penthouse. The vacation couldn't be over soon enough. As I ran through the crowded strip I knew one thing was for certain, I didn't want to see Tyler until we got back to Detroit. He had killed all hope, business was all there would be between us now.

♟ CHAPTER 16

Devynn sat in the back of Lace watching the crowd go crazy over one of their best girls, Purp, wiggling her ass with little effort from her hips. The club was packed for it to be the middle of the work week but Devynn wasn't tripping. The more thirsty niggas the better. She glanced around her and saw the bartenders pouring up drinks for a server to take to the VIP section of the strip club. Lace was a big thing in Detroit because unlike Amore, which was more business savvy. The doors to Lace opened to a wider range of clients. Lace wasn't Magic City, but the bitches working there were as cold as ice. They all ranged in colors and sizes giving Lace a sort of flavor needed to satisfy any man's taste. Lace saw its share of high rollers. Whenever anybody big came to town Lace was where they were especially on Saturday nights. It was definitely poppin' and Devynn was feeling the vibe. The music was bumping and every working girl was on the floor either popping their asses or their pussies in the faces of anybody with cash in their hands.

As the colored strobe lights flashed Purp had a large audience surrounding the stage while she pranced around dancing her heart out. Devynn stared at her and listened to the crowd go crazy when she lifted one of her legs up high, grabbed her ankle, and dropped into the splits. The stage filled with money and the bitch even picked up a few bills with the muscles of her ass cheeks; while bouncing up and down still doing the splits. Devynn's eyebrows raised impressed with the show Purp was putting on. She averted her eyes from the stage and from the table she was seated. With her drink she could barely make out Adrianna in the crowd. She was making conversation with a few men at a table who Devynn had noticed were being a little stingy with their wallets. She was smiling at them and laughing flirtatiously. Devynn smirked knowing what she was doing. Adrianna was a beautiful Latina woman, and very likable. It was hard to deny her any want or need; she just had that type of personality. She was like Poison Ivy. After a few more moments of talking to them Adrianna grabbed two Becky's, Bubbles and Candy, for the table of men to have fun with. Devynn knew that those girls were into some freaky shit. It was a definite whenever they were put on a job somebody's bank was going to get broken. Once they introduced themselves and made themselves at home on the laps of two of the men Adrianna began making her way towards the table Devynn was seated at. When she saw Devynn shaking her head she couldn't help the grin that spread across her face.

"Give them five minutes and I guarantee you them niggas are going to be emptying' every content in their pockets," she said proudly.

"Whateva," Devynn told her in her heavy New York accent popping a piece of gum in her mouth.

Adrianna shrugged her shoulders causing the half shirt she wore to raise and expose the golden sarcophagus forever branded on the side of her toned stomach.

"Where the fuck is Mocha's ass at?" Adrianna asked looking around the crowded club to see Mocha's familiar face.

"I don't know, I told her ass to come. You know she's on her own fuckin' time," Devynn leaned back in her seat ignoring the few eyes of men staring at her.

Devynn was one of the few gorgeous dark skinned women in the world. Her cheekbones were high, and although skinny like a model, she had a little something behind her to hold. Another drink appeared in front of Devynn unexpectedly. She just waived it away back to whatever low life nigga sent it. She sipped the drink she already had knowing that none of the thirsty niggas in that club would ever be lucky enough to take her home. Devynn's heart was cold as ice and because of that she wouldn't even entertain any of the men who had even enough guts to take whack at any type of relationship with her. The business she was in she knew dating anyone was risky, money was her only motive and if love never came she'd have a room full of diamonds to comfort her.

"Well hopefully she hurries the fuck up," Adrianna said the look on her face implying that Mocha needed to be there.

Devynn studied Adrianna's outfit and noticed that she was a little more dressy than usual. Instead of the usual skinny jeans on Adrianna's thick lower half she wore a pair of black leggings. On her feet were a pair of badass nude pumps that crossed at the ankles. Adrianna even had a little bit of makeup on her already naturally beautiful face.

"Is Ray going to be here?" Devynn asked and the tomato redness that overcame Adrianna's entire face was her answer. "I knew you liked that nigga. I see you checking him all the time. His dick must be something if it got you dressing for him."

"Shut up bitch, you don't know my life! No he's not going to be here!" Adrianna snapped but she knew instantly how untrue her statement was.

She and Devynn had been a team for four years before The Last Kings. Vinny found them, starving and hungry in the streets New York. At the time their only means of survival was hitting a few licks and sticking a few fuck niggas up. The money never lasted long with their lavish spending habits and they were often stuck in situations where they had to go without for days at a time. Vinny came into their lives and saved them and all he asked in return was loyalty. He had to be sure he could trust them so he gave them a target to hit. They had never killed anyone before, but for what he was offering them they would have taken anyone out of the game. After they successfully had removed the target Vinny took the two of them under his wing. They moved work underground in New York to not get the attention of the current boss of the city at that time, but did however infiltrate his cartel. Vinny needed the name of the connect and they got it. A short while after informing Vinny the name they heard that same name in the news. The man's body was found burnt to crisp in his Audi. There was suspected foul play but nothing was ever proven. The girls didn't ever ask what happened, but they knew then that the Italian Mafia was nothing to fuck with. When Vinny came to them with the proposition to be a part of maybe the biggest cartel known to the States. They hopped at the chance, money signs flashing before their hungry eyes. Their first meeting with Ray was a few weeks before the meeting at his home.

Devynn saw immediately the spark in Adrianna's eyes as they listened to Ray inform them of what they would be up against. Devynn herself couldn't deny that he was the epitome of a boss. He carried himself like he was made of money. When he spoke the education he harbored was the truth. It intrigued Adrianna because she had expected a hood nigga like the ones she'd dealt with in the past. She knew then why Vinny invested so much in Ray, at just that first meeting with him she had more faith in his operation then she'd had in anything for herself in her whole life.

"Mmmhmm," was all Devynn said. Normally she would have warned Adrianna about the decisions her heart made. But after two failed attempts at love she hoped her girl had grown some fuckin' sense. "D and Amann coming?" She asked Adrianna instead.

"They were supposed to have been here already too," Adrianna said the color slowly coming back to her face.

Devynn opened her mouth to speak but just as she did the three of them all sauntered into the club at the same time. One hell of a coincidence. Mocha walked in looking ravishing as always with her hair pulled back neatly into a ballerina bun and a skin tight black dress with the sides cut out. Her face held a smug expression. She knew she was late but she didn't care.

"Wassup?" D said once they were all at the table. "This muhfucka is popping tonight!"

"I don't give a fuck how popping it is, I'm missing out on money to be here," Amann looked at Adrianna with a look that could kill. "You think the nigga is gon' show?"

"I scoped the muhfucka out before we pulled in, I ain't see nobody suspicious," D said.

"When they ran in Taste it was real messy," Devynn said. "They were some amateur niggas, I'm not from here but I could tell they weren't from here either."

"You hear their voices?" Amann asked.

"Nah," Devynn shook her head. "But we need to figure out who the fuck these niggas are."

"No," Adrianna disagreed. "We need to figure out who sent them."

"The feds know what happened?" Mocha asked.

"Of course them muhfuckas know, you know somebody had to call their asses. By the time they got there though there weren't any bodies to be found and they didn't have a warrant to look around. We moved all the money here just until the drop is made."

"You know them niggas are mad," Mocha said.

"Yea," Devynn agreed. "But until Tyler comes back it's best not to get on their bad side."

"Do you think they might try and hit Lace?" Mocha asked Adrianna.

She hadn't even gotten the words out of her mouth before Adrianna nodded her head towards the door reaching for her waist. Entering the strip club was a banter of men ranging in all ages and they didn't look like they were there to enjoy in the festivities of half naked bitches prancing around. Nobody but the five people at the table noticed the newcomers and the crowd was so thick that it was hard to make all of them out, but Team Mula already knew what was up. The way the intruders moved through the crowd of people was snake like and Mocha could tell by the way they were dressed that Detroit wasn't their home. What niggas would wear Timberlands to the strip club in the summertime?

"A thirsty nigga can smell a dollar from a hundred miles away," Adrianna said standing to her feet.

"These niggas don't know who the fuck they're fuckin' with!" D exclaimed infuriated grabbing for the metal on his hip. "How the fuck they even get in?"

Before they knew what was happening the men dispersed covering all ground in the club and began opening fire. At first people thought it was a hoax and they cheered. But once bodies began dropping and blood splattering in the air the commotion began. The crowd became a frenzy of butt naked bitches and wanna be ballers frantically trying their best to get out of the club. All exits were covered so no one was going anywhere. They all split up and took cover as bullets rained all around us.

"Help!!"

"Oh my God!"

"I don't want to die man!"

There were several screams being let out as more bodies dropped.

"Get down!" Amann yelled to Mocha and he shot his pistol over her killing two of the shooters.

Fuck this, Mocha thought. She reached and grabbed the pistol she kept strapped to her thigh and began firing too.

"There they go!" she heard somebody yell but that didn't stop her from using her extended arm to dead them.

No mercy, she thought as she blew off the top of one of their heads close range.

Adrianna and Devynn were already on it too. Devynn had her twins out and Mocha witnessed her pistol whip a nigga and then blow his brains out all over Purp and Candy. The two of them were so scared they were trembling. Before Mocha could yell for them to get to their secured entry headquarters under the club half of Candy's head was blown off. Purp was so startled she jumped to her feet to run but her body soon was embedded with at least twenty rounds. Her body jerked on the ground trying to hold on to any little piece of life she had left. Team Mula held their ground until their own people finally got there and swarmed the club. The gun fight seemed to last forever until they finally seemed to realize that The Last Kings had them outnumbered. But by then it was too late, they hadn't thought their plan all the way through and it wasn't going to be over until all of them were dead. Devynn squeezed both of her triggers until they clicked, and when they were smoking she was finally able to hear that there were no more shots being fired. The strobe lights just gave that effect. She stood up and looked at the blood bath before her and saw there were at least fifty dead bodies, a few of their own laid out.

"Lets go!" D yelled to Mocha, Adrianna, Amann and Devynn.

Outside in the parking lot was almost as chaotic as the scene that had just taken place in the strip club. Cars were hopping curbs just to get the fuck out of there.

"It's only a matter of time before the feds get here," Mocha said pulling out her phone to call Ray. "Ain't no way a cleanup team can pull that shit off! It's like fifty dead muhfuckas in there!"

"I know," Amann stood back and shook his head. "We ain't got no choice but to let the shit ride."

"Si," Adrianna said. "I have to stay since I know them fuckin' pigs are going to need to speak to me. Devynn get Mocha home safe. Amann and D call Ray and let him know what's up. Tell him his blocks aren't safe and neither are any of his businesses, two in one day?"

"Something ain't right," Devynn said as they all walked quickly towards their vehicles leaving Adrianna behind.

Nobody said anything, but it was a fact that they all felt the same way.

"Today is drop off day...before everything hits Amore," Devynn continued. "Those niggas had to have known that...but—"

"Not one nigga made a move for the money," D finished for her.

Devynn nodded her head and Mocha shook hers.

"What were they trying to prove then?" Mocha asked opening the door to her BMW coupe.

"The way them niggas came in execution style said it all," Amann said over his shoulder getting into his Corvette parked on the opposite side of Mocha's vehicle. "They were trying to send a message. Of what? Now that's the question. I ain't recognize not one of them niggas."

They all nodded agreeing. Those men couldn't have been from Detroit, the city respected Ray too much to even dare to do that shit. But who?

"We about to go get at Ray and make this drop off. Lay low for a minute," D instructed. "Dev don't go home go to a hotel or some shit. I'm sending ten niggas with y'all, if you need us just call. We're going to get to the bottom of this shit."

Devynn nodded her head and hopped into the BMW with Mocha.

"Make sure Adrianna is straight too," she informed D.

"Already on it," he told her nodding to the parking lot across the street where three black Mercedes were parked almost unnoticeable in the night. "Be easy I'll get at you in the morning."

And with that he shut the door to the car. He knew Ray wasn't going to be too happy, but that was the least of his worries. His worry was that niggas had just started a war and they had no idea why.

♟ CHAPTER 17

K hiron pulled up to Amore and he couldn't help but to be impressed with the establishment. It was nothing he'd expected. The restaurant was two stories and the entire look of it expelled class. The parking lot was completely packed. From where he was parked he had a clear view of the inside of the restaurant. The lower lever consisted of filled dinner tables surrounding a large dance floor with couples swaying together slowly. Everyone inside that Khiron could see were in dress attire and he knew then that his black Armani suit was a good choice. Khiron fixed his collar slightly before stepping out of his vehicle and making his way to the entrance.

Inside Amore Ray was on the top level of Amore in the large secluded VIP balcony section. There were five huge men that surrounded him, ready to take bullets from all sides and not letting anyone get too close. But by the look on his face nobody would be bold enough to come his way. He was infuriated with the news he'd just received. Not one but two of his businesses had been hit in one day. It couldn't have been a coincidence he'd be a fool to think that.

"Fuck that shit. I want niggas on every block looking for the nigga that set that shit up!" Ray barked into the phone.

"Aight fam, but check this shit. Them niggas busted in here and never went for the money," Amann told him.

"What they want then?" Ray asked. "If it wasn't the money what the fuck them niggas want?"

"We don't know," Amann told him.

"Find out. Drop what was at Lace off here."

"Aight fam."

Ray disconnected the call with Amann and waited patiently for Khiron to arrive. He was angry at what Amann had told him, but even when a war was waging business had to continue. Ray watched as a light skinned kid with curly hair and impressive designer suit made his way towards where Ray was sitting. Before he could make it completely to the table he was stiff armed and stopped.

"Raise em'," one of Ray's personal body guards demanded preparing to check Khiron and strip him of any weapons.

Ray watched Khiron silently to see his reaction. The kid looked at the guards and then at Ray.

"This is your city, I respect that. But if this Fat Albert muhfucka don't move his arm in two seconds he won't have one to extend," the kid's voice was low but icy. "I'm here to conduct business, but I don't know you and personally I think it would be better if this thing stayed on my hip."

Ray chuckled shaking his head slightly and waived at his guard to let the kid through. He motioned for Khiron to sit down, which he did, and offered him a drink, which he declined.

"You got something for me?" Ray said cutting right to the chase.

"I wouldn't be here wasting your time if I didn't," Khiron told him.

Ray looked different from the last time he'd seen him. The last time Khiron saw him he thought he was in charge, now he knew.

"Five minutes," Ray told Khiron.

While Khiron was busy studying him, Ray patiently gathered his thoughts. In a day's time Ray found out all he needed to know about Khiron. He knew everything from where he lived all the way to which hand he wiped his ass with. He also knew that the reason Khiron was there seated in front of him in the first place was because he needed a connect. From the information Ray gathered Atlanta was a hungry city and Khiron was losing it. Tyler had over exaggerated the moves of the kid. Whereas he knew how to play the game he didn't know how to own it. You could only rule with an iron fist for so long before it turned on you.

"No need for a time stamp fam," Khiron said to Ray leaning in on the table. "You know why I'm here. If you know why I'm here that means you already have an answer for me."

Ray wanted to laugh at the boldness of the kid. He didn't speak; he just stared at the nigga before him. Fear was nonexistent in his eyes as he stared back at Ray awaiting an answer. There was something about Khiron that didn't sit right with Ray, but Ray couldn't quite put his finger on it. They hadn't been in each other's presence but five minutes, but it was true Ray had an answer ready for him before he even had entered his restaurant.

Khiron sat before Ray young and cocky which meant he already had two strikes against him. The only reason he decided to humor the nigga was because he came through Tyler. But unfortunately for Khiron the chair he sat in was as close as he would get to Ray's operation. Atlanta was a big market but losing Khiron's business would be but a small loss. He wouldn't ever make the mistake of allowing his product to be pushed through a place if he didn't approve of the man in charge. That's how the game got fucked up and how niggas got over. Ray took his time to speak, but when he did the meaning of his words was clear.

"I would ask you how you heard about me," Ray started while pouring himself a glass of Hennessey. "But I honestly don't give a fuck. You had it right though, this is my city." Ray raised his arms up halfway with his palms facing upward. "My establishment, my table…my chair," he motioned to Khiron's chair. "I'll give you a pass just because you're new in town, but had you been anyone else snapping? Ya brains would be falling from the sky like fuckin' confetti, feel me?"

Ray looked at the diamond Rolex shining on his wrist, and decided to speed up the process. It was like he was holding a job interview and he just wanted the nigga out of his office.

"You walked in here and made two mistakes. When my man says arms up, you don't speak. You do it. If he wants your guns," Ray insinuated that he knew Khiron was strapped heavy, "you drop em' on the table. I don't like that sassy shit, that's a trait of a bitch."

Ray saw Khiron's jaw clench and unclench and a vein pulsated on his right temple but he didn't say anything so Ray continued.

"Understand this my man," Ray took a gulp of his drink before staring so coldly into Khiron's eyes Khiron felt a chill go down his back. "My answer isn't just no. It's *fuck* no. You obviously didn't know shit about me when you made contact with my right hand but let me peep you on game. You never conduct business blinded. You hopped, skipped and took a leap of faith to my city on hope. The fuck did you think was going to happen here? You thought you were going to leave here a satisfied customer because what? What the fuck do you have to offer me? Money?" Ray scoffed.

"That's what this is about right?" Khiron asked through clenched teeth. Bottling his anger inside was getting harder by the second, Ray's words cut into him like spikes. Nobody had ever spoken to him like that since his father was alive and Ray wasn't his father.

"That's where you're wrong kid," Ray shook his head at the naivety. "Money can easily be spent, but in order for it to be made there has to be a strong foundation. Before I make any business moves I make it my business to know exactly who I'm dealing with. This shit is more than a sale to me. I don't give work to niggas just because they can afford it. My product will only be connected to success, unlike you, I did my research on the man I was meeting. The little operation you have going in ya city is too shaky to hold my shit."

Before Khiron could open his mouth to speak he was interrupted by a hand being placed on his shoulder.

He looked up and saw a middle aged Italian man standing over but not looking at him.

"That's your cue to leave," the Italian man said in a dismissive way. "We have actual business to conduct."

He studied the man's face and felt the blood rush from his. Khiron was looking dead into the face of the man who'd ordered the hit on his father. The notorious Vinny Mancini. Anger pulsated threw his veins and his hand twitched for the gun on his waist but when he saw one of the guards raise their eyebrow at him he decided to chill. Instead he stood up trying to remain professional and smirked at Ray.

"I'll be seeing you Ray," was all he said before he made his exit. "Real soon."

Bitch nigga, he thought walking away from the table.

He passed the entourage of Italian goons the Italian man brought with him. They all gave him looks as if to say he was beneath them. The meeting didn't go as he planned at all but Ray was wrong. Khiron would never go somewhere without knowing about his surroundings. Khiron knew more than what he would ever let on. Ray had no idea who he was fucking with. The one thing Khiron hadn't known was that he was working with the Italians but now that he knew he would be sure to tread lightly. He refused to meet the same sticky end his father did. Almost to the exit Khiron noticed a portrait hanging from one of the walls caught his attention. It was of two women and one of which he recognized right away. He was more than astonished to see Mocha hanging from the wall in front of him in the restaurant. The cream dress she wore brought out the mocha color of her skin and the smile on her flawless face held a secret. How did she know Ray? Why was her photo in his restaurant? He guessed there were a few things about her that he didn't know. The woman standing beside her had her arm linked in Mocha's and the word beautiful didn't do her justice. Her long hair flowed over her shoulders and her sharp brown eyes pierced the camera. Her red lips were turned in what was supposed to be a smirk. In the picture she wore a sophisticated form fitting red dress and although she faced forward he could see her ass from the front of her. There was something familiar about the girl but Khiron knew he'd never met her. A server was passing him and he stopped the young Italian woman before she went by.

"Who is this?" He asked not caring that he sounded rude. "Does she work here?"

The woman looked at him like he was crazy and laughed.

"Work here?" She shook her head. "That's Sadie, she runs this place."

Before Khiron could say another word she was gone, leaving him to stare at the picture for a few more moments.

"Sadie?" He said to himself and exited the restaurant.

There was something eating away at him while he stared at the photo. Then he remembered. She'd changed a lot but he could never forget her face. Fury engulfed him and he knew he had to get out of the restaurant before he left a trail of dead bodies. Enraged he pulled out his phone and dialed out once he was safe inside his vehicle.

"What the fuck happened Los?" he said once he heard "Hello."

"They all dead," the husky voice of one of his soldiers said.

Khiron knew that sending his men to Lace would be a suicide mission if the stories of the Last Kings presided them. He knew it would be enough to throw Ray off of his A game for their meeting. In the time it took Ray to pour his drink Khiron had already scoped out the men in wearing chef coats and hats going through a door that said "Authorized Personnel Only." That would have seemed normal had it not been for the fact that he scoped out the designer pants and shoes that poked out from under the chef coats. From where Khiron had been seated he had the perfect view of the lower level.

"But fam there's something else you need to know," Los said.

"What's that?"

"Ya girl, Mocha, she was there. She's one of them fam, she was one of the muhfuckas popping our people nigga."

The realization hit Khiron then, hard. It was like a punch in the face. He thought he was a good liar, keeping his business dealings away from her keen nose but Mocha in fact took the cake. He was hurting in his city while that bitch was living like a fucking queen in hers. He never once questioned the designer that forever laced her body or how she could easily afford to hop on a plane to come see him whenever. When he thought about it out of all the bitches he'd fucked with Mocha was the only one he didn't have to give a stack of bills to go shopping. She carried herself like a bad bitch but in all reality she was a boss. She was a part of the expanding underground drug cartel that was obviously blossoming with the help of the Italians. He should have known the Italians were a factor when he realized Ray owned Amore. The Italians were the enemy, Ray and the Italians were business partners. Ray was the enemy. Ray was the leader of The Last Kings. Mocha was a Last King...Mocha was the enemy. With that knowledge Khiron also knew one other thing. He'd had the key all along; the person who would open the door to the downfall of Detroit's underground kings.

"A'ight," was all Khiron said trying to swim through his ocean of thoughts. "What's going on now?"

"They moved it," Los said referring to the money that had been at Lace.

"Where?" Khiron asked but before he got an answer he watched a Corvette pull up to the valet parking of the restaurant.

Two men exited the vehicle each holding a fat suitcase and Khiron couldn't help the smile coming to his face. He disconnected the call and gave himself a silent praise. Way before Khiron made his trip into Detroit he sent a handful of niggas before him to watch the movements of Ray's operation. After a few weeks of surveillance Khiron had to admit that nigga Ray was smooth. His operation was flawless and he'd never seen another like it. The Last Kings was a force not many could fuck with, but still the men Khiron sent were able to figure out when the drop off days and times were. The point of the run ins that he'd formulated wasn't ever to rob him at that time. He knew Ray ran a handful of businesses and hitting them all would be too much work. But what Khiron did know was that with the thought of potentially getting robbed came a sense of security. Ray would want all of his money on lockdown and in one place. Seeing the Corvette pull up Khiron knew his theory had been correct. The theory being that Ray would move all of the money to the safest place he could think of until it was ready to be placed. As a hustler himself he knew how risky depositing large amount of drug money in the bank was, Ray needed to clean it first. Khiron's original plan was to conduct business and obtain a connect while robbing him blind. But after the way Ray spoke to him and seeing the portrait in the restaurant his plans had changed. A sickening smile came to his face, he wasn't going to rob the Ray of the money sitting inside of Amore, but now he knew where the heart of the whole operation was located.

It was no longer business, it was personal. Khiron was going to kill each and every one of those Italian bitches. Since Vinny's bullet was the one that pierced his father's skull he would get it the worst. Khiron's blood raged when he thought about how that piece of shit had touched him. Only one word pumped through his brain. Revenge. He picked up his phone called Mocha.

"Hello?" she answered her voice sounded exhausted.

"What up bae, where you at?" Khiron asked trying his best to keep the disgust from his voice.

"Nothing just watching some TV," Khiron shook his head at how easily the lie rolled off her tongue.

"My plane just touched down," he lied. "Meet me at my hotel in a few hours."

He heard her sit up straight through the phone.

"You're here?" he heard a mixture of concern and excitement in her voice.

"Yea bae, I wanted to surprise you," he lied again. "I tied up a few loose ends in the A and thought it was time for a little venture into my wifey's city. See how she's living."

His last words had an icy effect to them but Mocha barely took notice.

"Ok, um text me what hotel and the room number. I have some shit to handle right now but a few hours sounds like a plan," her voice dropped as if she didn't want anyone around her to hear the plans she was making.

"Aight ma, I'ma see you," and with that Khiron disconnected the call only to make one last dial out.

His eyes stayed on the Corvette until the two men returned to the vehicle. They didn't know it, but that night would be their last night on the earth alive. It was true that Detroit was Ray's city and he ran it out of love instead of fear, but it was Khiron's game and when he was done with the last kings his name would shake the bravest of hearts. He was going to wreak havoc and torture them all. He'd vowed long ago that his father's death wouldn't be in vein. The shit at Lace and the hair salon was nothing compared to what he had in store for all them muhfuckas. When he saw the car prepare to pull off he made one last phone call and began to tail behind it.

"Let the war begin."

♟ CHAPTER 18

W hat was that about?" Vinny asked Ray once the two shook hands.

Ray leaned back in his seat and smirked.

"Business as usual," he shrugged. "Little niggas always approaching for work but can't even deliver."

Vinny stared at the man before him and chuckled at his suave. Ray was no longer the kid with potential he'd met with in the back seat of a Mercedes. He knew that investing in Ray would be good for business but in all actuality Ray had invested in him. Vinny was in awe at the way Ray had branched off of him. Ray was the connect to six major drug demanding cities, so in turn Vinny was all of their connect. The drug demand was so high that if Vinny didn't want to conduct business with anyone *but* Ray again he would never have to. The Italian drug cartel was making millions off of one operation and that was why in Vinny's eyes Ray had rightfully earned the title of a king.

Ray asked Vinny to have a seat but he declined.

"Business as usual," he said but in so many words he was telling Ray that he was just there to pick up and get out.

"Aight," Ray said nodding his head. "It's all here. Miami, DC, LA, Chicago, Houston, and New York. Two mil."

Vinny raised his eyebrow at Ray's carelessness but didn't say anything. He trusted Ray's judgment and he also knew that Amore was the safest place for the money. He nodded to his men to go grab it and shook Ray's hand once more before he too made his exit. That was the way Vinny was, he was never in one spot for more than twenty minutes. He also never went anywhere without an army of Italians behind him and an automatic pistol.

Ray rubbed his facial hair and looked at the phone sitting on the table. He had no doubt in his mind that his generals would handle the little situation that took place that night, but when it came down to it he knew he needed both his left and right hand. Something told him that the fuckery would continue and that somebody was sending him a message. Ray was lowkey glad that his two leading generals would be touching down in the morning the horrendous scent of an upcoming war was frozen at the tip of his nose.

♟ CHAPTER 19

After that night in the restaurant things between me and Tyler were a little awkward but we tried to make the best of our arrangement. We went on many tours and adventured off a lot by ourselves. No matter how hard I tried I couldn't bring myself to be evil to him, although he'd broken my heart twice. I didn't know if it was love or the simple fact that I respected his loyalty to the game. He was right after all. Mixing business with pleasure never worked, and I knew the life span of a hustler was short. Instead of indulging in the negatives I decided to shoot for positives with Tyler. He surprised me our last night in the beautiful place and something in the air changed between us.

"You can't just tell me what it is?" I asked him pouting as I tried to keep my balance on the sand.

"Then it wouldn't be called a 'surprise' ma," Tyler smiled at me and grabbed a hold of my waist assisting me with walking.

"Well you could have at least told me we were going to the beach," I cut my eyes at him holding his arm lightly. "I wouldn't have put the fuckin' red bottoms on. My shoes are going to be ruined!"

"Chill Say, plus you have about a hundred more pairs where those came from," he laughed.

Before I could say anything else smart we came up on the most beautiful beach scene I'd ever seen in my life. It was like a movie. On the beach, overlooking the water a single table with a white table cloth and two chairs was set up. On the table were two plates with covers over them, two wine glasses, and a candle in the center. Around the table rose petals were scattered and a piano, yes a fucking piano, played soft tunes into the night.

"Tyler," I said breathlessly and stopped in my tracks. "Is all that..?"

"For you?" Tyler stood in front of me and grabbed my hands. "Yes. It's our last night in paradise and I wanted to do something special for you ma."

"Like an apology?" I pressed my luck.

"Real niggas," he said, "don't apologize. But they do make up for their wrongs."

"Like an apology," I said matter of factly and he laughed.

"Shut up and come on," he pulled me towards the table.

He pulled me chair out for me and when I sat he pushed me back in. When he joined me on the opposite side of the table he wore a huge kool aid smile.

"What?" I asked feeling myself blush at the way he was looking at me.

"You look gorgeous," was all he said.

I rolled my eyes not wanting to get the wrong idea again.

"Hungry?" He asked me.

"Hell yea," I said and felt my stomach growl, "What's on the menu?"

"Oh nothing," Tyler said smugly lifting both of our tops off of our plates. "Just some macaroni and cheese, fried chicken, black eyed peas, and cornbread."

The aroma filled my nostrils and I was in heaven. The sight of the food made my mouth water, it looked absolutely scrumptious!

"My favorite!" I exclaimed in shock. "How'd you know?"

After the question was out I realized how dumb it sounded. Tyler probably knew me as well as Ray did. It didn't hit me until then that I barely knew anything personal about the man I thought I loved.

"It's not as good as Grandma Rae's but I tried," Tyler shrugged.

It touched me slightly that he'd gone to such great lengths to make my last night there paradise, but then I had to stop myself before I got to thinking too much.

This is why Ray sent him, he's just doing his job, I told myself.

"Thank you," I said and dug into my plate not able to stop.

He was right it was nothing like Grandma Rae's but it was still delicious. We ate until our stomachs were full and I could see a little pudge in my Dolce dress.

"I didn't know you could cook," I told him wiping my mouth on a napkin.

"There's a lot you don't know about me ma," he said and pushed his empty plate away from him. "When I was young my mom was always gone. So I had to learn to take care of home myself."

I nodded my head knowing how that was. I could see why he and Ray were best friends.

"Tell me about yourself Tyler, there's a lot I don't know. But I would like to," I told him in all honestly.

"There's not enough time in the world for my story Say," Tyler chuckled. "Just know we all got a story and right now mine is here. With you."

"Make time then," I said not wanting to let him off that easy.

I knew that was probably the only time I'd get him alone again. Once we got back to Detroit it would be all business and no play once again. The Sadie in Jamaica and the Sadie in Detroit were two separate people and I knew the same held true for Tyler, I wanted to get the most out of it. Since the incident at the restaurant no longer did my clit throb for Tyler's presence but when he was away I still did miss him. I didn't want to go back to Detroit and it's the same way, because he'd be away a lot longer than thirty minutes. If I couldn't have him as my man, lover, or whatever I would settle for whatever piece of him he would give. When I said I wanted to know him I meant it. Tyler looked at me confusion on his face.

"I promise I won't ever make any type of advance on you again," I said placing my chair directly on the right of his and sitting in it. "This is our last night here, so if I'm not going to get any dick you have to give me something."

I shrugged placing my elbow on the table and placing my head in my hand. I'd kept it one hundred with him and I was expecting the same in return. He studied my face intently to see if I was serious.

"Aight ma, since you insist. What do you wanna know?" He asked.

"Everything," I stated simply and Tyler paused again.

"Here's the shortened version. I was born in Detroit and raised by a mother who worked three jobs just to keep a roof over my head. My old man was an abusive alcoholic but once I turned fifteen all that shit stopped. I almost killed that nigga after he beat my moms so bad she had a broken jaw and rib cage," he stopped but I didn't interrupt, I wanted him to continue. "I started hustling at eighteen with Ray just getting it how we lived. I came up, fast. We always had a business plan. The Last Kings started with us. I don't know if he ever told you that, but this shit popped off long before Coopa ran the city. Shit was coo for a while, my mom only had to work one job since I was taking care of the bills and shit. Everything was going good until some hating ass niggas got wind of our money chase and did a drive by one our house. Unfortunately for them I wasn't there, but unfortunately for me my moms was. She was in the middle of cooking dinner when the shots hit her body, my little sister was upstairs in her bed sleep. Didn't even know what happened."

"Tyler I'm so sorry," I said sitting up straight. "I didn't know."

"It's good shorty," Tyler shook his head the look in his eyes distant. "I found out who did it and sent all their body parts to their mothers in little freezer bags."

I'd forgotten the illusion that Jamaica had given me of Tyler and I was false. It was true that he could be sweet but that's because we were on the same team. At heart Tyler was a cold blooded killer, it came with the job description. Mercy wasn't even a word to him, it didn't exist.

"How is Marie by the way?" I asked knowing he kept his little sister's whereabouts lowkey. I knew she had to be about eighteen now though.

"Good," Tyler smiled at the thought of his little sister. "A lot like you actually."

"That's not a good thing," I smiled.

"Who says?" Tyler held my gaze deeply and I had to avert his gaze.

"Have you ever been in love Tyler?" I asked the sand.

"I've had my share of bitches, but no I can't say I've ever loved one of em'. In the life I'm living there honestly isn't enough time for it."

I nodded at his answer slightly relieved that no woman had ever captured his heart.

"What about you?" he asked catching me off guard.

"Have I ever been in love?" I repeated the question and thought about the pain I'd suffered as a young teenager with my mother's devil. "No, I've never let a man get that close to me. I've never even allowed myself to have a real boyfriend. Bosses don't have time for pain."

I answered the question trying not to think about my past trauma, but the sound of my own screams invaded my mind and I couldn't stop the tears from flowing. I removed myself from the table and went to stand by the piano facing the water. Gasping for air I tried to calm myself down. Through my long wet eyelashes I could barely see the moon reflecting off of the water. Tyler's presence was soon felt behind me and I tried to stop the tears kept coming, nobody but Mocha had ever seen me cry.

"Sadie what's wrong, ma?" Tyler asked grabbing my shoulders and pulling me to him but I couldn't speak.

That one question sent me diving deep into the memories I'd tried so hard to erase. All I could see was Nino's face as he mounted me and took the only thing I'd ever had to offer. Nino was the reason I bled every time when I first started having sex on my own free will. Nino was the reason why I'd never trusted any man besides Ray. Nino was the reason why my feelings for Tyler were so fucking jumbled. How could I love a man when I had no idea what the fuck love was? How could any man love a woman like me? I had too much baggage and that was why whenever any relationship of mine seemed to be blooming I did something on purpose to end it. Ending any connection between me and that person…it was the only thing I could control. That way I didn't feel the pain. But right there on that beach? I felt it. I felt it all.

"Tyler just let me go!" I yelled trying to fight him off a sea of emotions swarming me.

But he didn't. We fell into the sand and he held me through every sob, stroking my hair and telling me it would be alright. Whatever it was, it would be alright. When I was finally done I wiped my eyes and turned to face him.

"I'm so sorry," I told him and he cupped my face in his hands. "I didn't mean to ruin another dinner."

"It's coo ma," concern drenched his face. "What's going on?"

I studied him. A real ass nigga, a dying breed. In that split second I knew I could trust him. I told him everything, about the rapes, how I was forced to hustle and how I came to stay with Grandma Rae. He never once interrupted me, when I told him about the rapes I'd never seen him look so mad before. The vein on his temple pulsated violently and when I was done I begged him not to tell Ray. I couldn't bare the thought of Ray knowing about the skeletons in my closet. He promised me and held me again.

"If that nigga wasn't already dead; I'd send an army of niggas to blow every one of his fuckin' limbs off ma," he said into my hair. "I swear on my life no man will ever hurt you again. They're going have to get through me first. You hear me?"

He lifted my chin with his finger and I looked deeper into his eyes. I could see that not only did my story make him angry but there was pain there too. He hurt because I hurt. Something deep inside me erupted and I knew then, at that moment that my feelings for that man weren't faux. I nodded my head because I believed him with every fiber of my being.

"I love you Tyler," I was able to breathe just before he kissed me.

♟ CHAPTER 20

D evynn was livid as she waited a little after two o-clock for Tyler and Sadie to emerge from the large crowd of people exiting the airport. She leaned on her newly washed red Audi barely able to keep her balance. Anger coursed through her but the pain she felt almost knocked her off of her feet. Although in a pair of shorts and Diamond Supply t-shirt. She was still hot and patience was running low. When she finally spotted their smiling faces the look she wore instantly wiped their smiles from existence. There was a different glow on Sadie's normally serious face but she didn't acknowledge it when they approached her. She had news to tell them that would ground them but she knew that the airport was not the place to reveal such news. She also knew that Tyler had something like a temper and all the people exiting the airport to meet loved ones one minute might be laid out on the ground dead the next.

Tyler wasn't a dumb nigga he knew instantly something was up. There was a sadness so powerful in Devynn's eyes he knew something horrible had happened. Devynn was the type of bitch that never showed emotion, she was taught to be hardened to the core.

"Even in the worst pain of your life never show a nigga that you feel *anything*," was something she was known for saying.

Tyler and Sadie exchanged glances and seeing that Devynn shielded her eyes with her Ray Bans. Tyler waited until they pulled off from the airport to say anything.

"What the fuck is up?" he asked her looking at her from the passenger seat.

Devynn took a breath before she spoke.

"While you niggas been enjoying ya fun in the sun and shit," Devynn started her voice wavering slightly, "muhfuckas been here wilding off their asses. They hit Lace and the Salon."

Sadie leaned towards the front from the backseat. Devynn recapped the story for the two of them since they were the only ones missing in action. Sadie was hot, it read all over her face.

"Why the fuck didn't Ray call me?" she fumed. "I would have fuckin been here!"

"Chill Sadie," Tyler tried to calm her. He studied the way Devynn gripped the steering wheel as she drove on the highway and he knew there was more to the story that she hadn't said yet. "What's going on now Dev? They get the niggas that did the shit, cause if not on God I'ma handle that."

Devynn shook her head and gripped the steering wheel even harder. They couldn't see but tears were forming in her eyes.

"Now..." she started but choked up letting tears that had been nonexistent for five years roll down her face.

"Talk nigga!" Tyler barked at her.

"Amman and D are dead!" Devynn yelled pulling over on the highway. She got out and slammed her door.

"Fuuuck!" she screamed at the on looking cars and put her hands on her naturally curly afro.

A look of shock was frozen on both Tyler and Sadie's faces but soon Tyler's brow furrowed and the rage in his whole body language. His bros couldn't be dead. Nah, not Amann and D. Those niggas were survivors, real soldiers. The Last Kings was created before them, but could never be the same after them. Never. He and Sadie both hopped out after Devynn and went to stand before her as she screamed. Tyler reached out and snatched the sunglasses off of her face before gripping her shoulders. He needed to see the lie in them, but when he didn't he let her go rubbing his chin and shaking his head.

"Nah," he couldn't believe it.

They had all come from different backgrounds, but the operation had pulled them all close knit together. They all had each other's backs. Or that's how it was supposed to be.

"They're dead," Devynn said through clenched teeth. "As in hearts stopped. As in their bodies were found in D's Corvette this morning. And Ty, yo, their fucking heads were strapped in car seats behind em'! These niggas are fuckin' sick B!"

Sadie went to Devynn and held her as she sobbed. Just like Tyler had done her.

"Whoever did it carved some shit on their chests . It said 'None of you or yours are safe.' Amann saved my life Say! If it wasn't for that nigga I'd be dead grass and now look at him!" Devynn couldn't control her rogue emotions.

Tyler stood anguished watching the women cling to one another. The Last Kings didn't start shit with nobody; the money was the only motive. Tyler knew the game, the deaths of D and Amann meant that someone had just started a war and so far they were losing. Whoever had ordered the hits was like a phantom, or at least that's what he got from Devynn's story. He knew it was something to worry about if Ray had no clue who the fuck was behind the madness. What he did know though was that the message was clear. The nigga was coming at their necks. Now that they knew to watch their backs it would be hard to catch them slipping again. There was only one person on his mind, and although no one knew her whereabouts but him he knew to never under estimate his enemy.

"Get me to my car Dev," he ordered. "Get Say to Ray's and I'ma be there later. I gotta go get Marie."

♚ CHAPTER 21

Tyler pulled into the apartment complex that he had set his sister up in. It was in a nice community shielded by a neighborhood of houses in the suburbs. He liked it because in order to get to it you had to know exactly where you were going. Tyler knocked on the apartment door on the first floor that was hers and waited for her to open it.

"Come in!" the soft voice of a woman said from the other side.

Tyler entered the apartment with a grim look on his face. A beautiful skinny young woman was perched on a leather couch wearing silk Gucci pajamas smiling at him. She too was light skinned with soft short curly hair and hazel eyes. Her cheekbones were high and her nose sharp, she was the female version of Tyler.

"What I tell you about locking that door?" he said as his greeting to his baby sister.

"Well hello to you too nigga," she extended a weary eye. "The fuck are you doing here anyway? I'd think you'd be resting after your little vacation."

She asked that like Tyler didn't stop by frequently just to make sure she was straight. But he'd already stopped by a few times that week and he always called before he just showed up. Something was up, she could tell by the look in his eye. She could read her brother like a book.

"Put some clothes on, we gotta go," he said simply like her whole life wasn't inside of that large one bedroom apartment. To him though all of that shit was replaceable, her life wasn't. "Grab what you need and meet me in the car."

Marie wanted to protest but she knew better. Even if she did she saw the livid expression on her big brother's face and knew her words wouldn't do much of anything but stall time. She'd just gotten settled into her apartment and knew it was a mistake on her behalf due to the fact that she'd bounced around from place to place since a young age.

Tyler planned on moving Marie into Ray's estate until shit blew over and until they knew who was starting a war with them. There would be security and watchful eyes day and night, he couldn't bare the thought of losing his baby sister like he lost his mother. He'd been good about separating his street life and his relationship with his sister. He took her out of the hood just so she wouldn't be subjected to that life. He vowed to do any and everything to protect the small piece he had left of his family. Marie was a strong woman and although she'd never toted a gun, stared into the eyes of a dying man, or touched a kilo of cocaine but she understood the game. Wherever she went she was treated like a princess just because of who her brother was and who he was affiliated with. In every department store she was waited on hand and foot. She had her own car but Tyler insisted on her being chauffeured around in a bullet proof limousine if she ever needed to go anywhere. Her face was rarely seen on the streets, but when it was Tyler made sure she always wore a smile.

Marie stood up to get dressed but came to an abrupt stop at the sound of several cars screeching to a stop outside of her living room window. Running to the window Tyler glanced out and saw several men dressed casually hop out of three black Jeeps guns drawn. Marie saw them too and a look of terror crossed her face. Tyler cursed himself because he and Ray were the only ones who knew of her whereabouts which meant he must have been followed.

"Ty," Marie whispered behind him.

"Be easy sis," he turned to her knowing they didn't have much time. "Take this, we getting out of this bitch."

He handed her a 9 mm pistol glad he'd taught her how to use it, though he hoped she'd never have to. Several shots rang out and the two dropped to the floor in sync but no bullets came into the apartment. Ray found out what they had lit up when he looked back outside of the window. His Mercedes sat on four flats, all the windows were shot out, and the hood of the car was a blaze of fire. He saw the men taking cover just in time to grab Marie and run to the front door. Behind them the explosion of the car was so powerful the living room windows shattered and Ray shielded Marie's body from the glass and debris.

"Come on!" he ordered.

He exited the apartment first, gun raised. When he saw nobody in the hallway he took Marie by the hand and ran towards the staircase in the back of the apartment. He'd cased the apartment before he moved Marie into it so he knew there was a window on the third floor that overlooked the swimming pool of the complex. It was their only bet especially since he knew exit doors were out of the question. He knew the building was probably surrounded. Marie tried her best to keep up knowing that if she so much as stumbled they were dead. Behind her she heard a door open just as they turned to rush up the first flight of stairs and out of sight. Her heart pounded violently in her chest and feet moved faster than they ever had before. She knew that if her brother was running something bad as going down.

"They ain't in here! Raid this mu'fucka!" a deep voice echoed throughout the apartment building. "That was Tyler's car in the parking lot. They're here somewhere."

"Tyler where are we going?" Marie panted to her brother as they ran up the third flight of stairs.

Tyler ignored her and continued running as fast as his Retro Laker 6's would take him never once letting go of her hand. If it had just been him alone in the apartment he would have gone out blazing with the niggas, but his brotherly intuition kicked in. Keeping Marie safe was his only purpose at that point in time. Finally they reached the window on the third floor and Ray shot it out.

"We have to jump," he told her tucking his gun away and picking her up like a baby. He kissed her on the cheek. "Don't be scared," he whispered into her ear after seeing her eyes widen.

He stepped up and jumped just as the footsteps coming up the stairs after them got closer. Marie cringed and gripped Tyler's neck as they dropped from the third floor towards the pool. Marie gasped for air just before the water hit her body. The impact of the water was more than just painful but Tyler refused to let go of his sister. They sunk towards the bottom of the pool briefly but the presence of bullets hitting the water forced power into Tyler's long legs and he kicked his hardest until they surfaced. Around him he saw that the water no longer was clear, but stained red as innocent bystanders trying to enjoy a day at the pool became victims in a man hunt. They acted as shields for Ray and Marie when they exited the pool in a coughing frenzy.

"G-go!" Tyler coughed at Marie once they'd emerged from the pool with drenched and heavy clothes.

The pool area was chaotic with people screaming frantically pushing each other trying to get through the exit gat. Tyler and Marie ducked and dodged bullets but saw many people drop dead around them. A woman Marie recognized and her infant son lay dead and bloody in a pool chair but Marie focused on the purse that lay next to her. She made a quick dash to the purse and snatched it up, it was her turn to lead Ray.

"This way! She never parked in the parking lot!" Marie yelled back at Tyler pushing through the crowd trying to get through.

The sight of the gun in her hand made people scatter clearing a way for her and Tyler to run through. Marie rummaged through the woman's purse until she found a cell phone, the garage door opener and car keys. She then tossed the purse onto the ground and lead Tyler to the garaged that matched the number on the garage door opener. She'd pressed the button way before they got there and they wasted no time hopping in the beat up Toyota Camry. Their clothes soaked the cloth interior and Tyler reversed like a mad man out of the garage. He sped the opposite way out of the complex glad the car at least had tinted windows. In order to exit the complex completely he had to double back around and pass the parking lot, which was nothing but a sight of fire and smoke due to Tyler's still burning Mercedes. His eyes zoomed in on the Jeeps the niggas had hopped out of and focused on the personalized license plates. Personalized license plates meant that the vehicles weren't rentals. Atlanta read clear as day. The niggas were from Atlanta. Ray had just denied the city's boss business with The Last Kings.

"Damn," Tyler said whipping out of the complex and through the suburb neighborhood.

He knew who was behind the bloodshed in the city. What was even more fucked up was that he was the one who'd welcomed him into Detroit by even responding to his phone call. He reached into his pocket for his phone but realized upon looking at the water damaged device it was of no use.

"Hand me that phone Marie," he said taking his eyes off the road as they passed an intersection in the neighborhood. He had to call Ray ASAP and let his boy know what was good.

To the right of him he saw that traffic had a stop sign but he saw too late that the big black truck headed straight for them had no intentions of stopping. Before they knew what had hit them Marie's side of the car was violently rammed causing Tyler to lose control of the vehicle. Marie's screams were deafening and Tyler tried and failed to regain control of the car. They spun out until they crashed into a tree. Marie's head had hit the dash board so there was blood trickling down her face and Ray was pinned to the steering wheel. He tried to reach his gun when he saw the group of niggas running towards the vehicle, but it was no use.

"Marie," he said to his sister who's tears were mixing into the blood streams on her cheeks. "No!"

Her window was busted out and a hand grabbed her by her short hair yanking her through the window.

"No! No!" she tried to fight wriggling her body and kicking her feet but they were too strong for her.

"Contain that bitch!" a voice said but she couldn't focus on the face.

Her vision was getting blurry, the trauma of her head injury was causing her to blackout. The last thing she saw while she was being carried swiftly away to the big black truck was a gun being aimed at her brother's head. One last tear dropped from her eye and she blacked out but not before she heard the bullet that ended her brother's life.

♟ CHAPTER 22

Khiron sat on the large King sized bed inside the room of his penthouse suite watching Mocha move her body seductively before him. The lights were dim she turned around exposing the way her ass ate up her thong just before she began making it clap. No music played, she rocked to her own beat. All she wanted to do was please her man and forget about all of the chaos in her life. With Amann and D's double funeral the next day she needed something to drown out the pain of losing two men she'd come to think of as her brothers. It was her second night with Khiron and she noticed he'd been real distanced but she knew a little of her loving would bring him back to her.

Khiron was toying with Mocha, playing her like a game of chess. He just needed his next move to be his best move. Manipulation was the game and he needed it to be in his favor. He wanted nothing more than to put a bullet in her head but what use would her corpse be to him? Her smooth mocha skin and plumped ass enticed him and he felt his manhood grow three more inches. Khiron couldn't lie, he loved Mocha. Women of course caught his attention in the past, but no one but she was able to catch his heart. That made the betrayal he felt all the more worse. It caused him some grief to know that she would have to die with the rest of her team. He had a small army of niggas just waiting for the word, but the thing was Mocha hadn't given him anything. He sighed and shook his head. He had to speed up the process. His operation couldn't wait for him to get his nut off. He needed to formulate a plan before Ray traced the deaths of the two men he killed to him. Khiron was ruthless in the head. He didn't give a fuck and never did. He felt nothing when he cut off their heads with the sharpened machete. It was refreshing to him. All of them would die gruesome deaths, and when he got to the Italians he would do the same to them. He was crazy as hell for going at the Italian cartel but he knew killing The Last Kings would send him a message. Nino's legacy was not to be fucked with.

"Bring that ass here," he bit his lip at her and she smiled sashaying his way.

"Mmm, you ready for me already?" Mocha said seductively straddling him.

"Nah chill ma," Khiron placed him hands on her waist stopping her from grinding on him. He knew he wouldn't be able to stop her once she got going. "I just wanna kick something to you right quick."

Mocha cocked her head at him and eyed him with her light brown eyes curious as to what he had to say.

"Well speak nigga," Mocha told him. "This pussy can't wait all day."

Khiron thought quickly about his plan knowing that everything about it was pointing against him but putting Mocha in the know was the only way she would sing information. If it didn't work it would be nothing to just put her to sleep forever in that hotel suite.

"I know about you ma," Khiron started and immediately saw the look on her face go from pleasured to nervous.

"Know about me," Mocha giggled trying to catch herself. "I would hope you knew me, you've been fuckin' with me for a while now bae. Now come here and make me feel good."

"Nah Mocha," Khiron pushed her hands off of him. "You know what I mean. The Last Kings ring a bell?"

Mocha's face paled and she stood to her feet.

"Were you ever going to tell me?" Khiron asked her seriously wanting that answer.

"No," Mocha didn't even have to think before she answered and that made Khiron even more angry than when he got wind of who she really was.

Mocha saw the anger in Khiron's face and couldn't help not giving a damn. She didn't feel that Khiron needed to know about her business dealings. It wasn't any of his business, she also didn't inform him of her affiliation in fear that he would try and use her connections for his own personal gain. She felt something in the air change between them and she didn't like or trust it. She knew about Khiron. She wouldn't have kept visiting him in Atlanta if she didn't do some kind of research. His body count stretched a long way. He'd killed mercilessly to obtain his spot as Atlanta's boss so she knew that he was nobody you wanted to go toe to toe with. Khiron just nodded his head.

"I met with Ray a few nights ago," Khiron's intentions were no longer to keep his words sweet. He wanted to cut her deep to the core. "That nigga, he's a true boss I'm not going hate on em'. But every boss gets caught slipping right?"

Mocha stopped dressing herself and stared at Khiron in only a pair of shorts and her bra. The mood had been killed for her and her mindset was changing from girlfriend Mocha to Last King Mocha. The man before her was not the man she loved, the look in his eyes held something completely different. It was the look of a hungry dog.

"The fuck are you talking about Khiron? The Last Kings don't get caught slipping, least of all Ray so quiet that noise."

Khiron stood up and walked slowly to the night stand beside his bed. From it he pulled out a machete. The same machete he used to kill D and Amann in fact, it still was stained with their dried up blood.

"I'm assuming that's what those other two niggas thought? Right?" He smirked at Mocha and her mouth dropped.

"Y-you?" Mocha's mind reeled looking at the weapon. "You killed my bros?!"

Khiron's connect was just sent to prison and he just said he had a meeting with Ray. She remembered Adrianna mentioning something about a meeting with someone from Atlanta that he turned away. Mocha didn't really pay her any mind since Ray had a lot of business meetings. Standing there she wished she'd paid more attention and didn't leave her gun in the car. She backed up as far as she could until her back was pressed up against the wall and Khiron advanced on her.

"What do you want Khiron?" She asked him. "Why did you kill them?!"

"I want it all," Khiron smiled knowing his answer answered both questions. "I'm going to kill anyone in the way of what's mine."

In Khiron's crazy way of thinking Ray's operation was rightfully his since it was given to him by his father's killers.

"No!" Mocha cried out. "You bitch! You didn't come here to see me...you're trying to take the city; our city."

"Yea," Khiron shrugged. "Pretty much, and you're going to help."

"Fuck you," Mocha tried to make a dash for the door but Khiron grabbed her forcefully by her neck.

Mocha was a fighter, but her punches did nothing to Khiron's big build. Her energy was fading along with her breath so she stopped fighting after a few seconds. Khiron pinned her back up against the wall but as he opened his mouth to speak his phone vibrated with a message. Knowing what it was about he glanced at it, smiled, and turned his attention back to the woman he was suffocating.

"I don't want to kill you Mocha, but I swear to God I will," Khiron's voice was like venom and Mocha's body was paralyzed.

She felt hot tears coming to her eyes as she gulped for air. She stared into the cold eyes of the man she once loved and felt nothing but hatred. She saw her life flash before her eyes when his grip around her neck tighten and then loosen.

"I know you Mocha. You're not a hustler and you're not a killer. You kind of just fell into this profession and I want to take you out. Your place is beside the man in charge," Khiron decided to change up his approach. "I'm so sorry babe, I don't want to hurt you. You know I love you ma, but this is business. A woman of your caliber shouldn't have to work ever, help me ma. I promise I got you."

Mocha's mind was reeling. Her loyalty was to the Last Kings and a part of her wanted to spit in his face for what he was implying she do. But another part of her had to admit that he was right. The cartel was and had always been Sadie's idea; Mocha was just ride or die. But now faced with the presence of death she knew she wasn't ready to perish. The lavish life she lived came with a price and with every heart her bullets pierced a piece of her soul left her body. She felt like a traitor, she said she would go to the grave for her team. The tattoo branded on her body made that promise, but promises were meant to be broken. After the deaths of D and Amann the pain she felt was unbearable and feeling the tears trailing down her face she knew the Last Kings would never be the same. She knew she only had seconds to make her decision…so she did.

"Just promise me one something," Mocha choked on her tears and closed her light brown eyes. "And I'll do whatever you want."

Khiron felt the sticky smile forming slowly on his face.

"Name it ma," he wiped the tears from her face like he wasn't the one causing them.

"Sadie lives," Mocha's eyes shot open and there was a fire so strong in them Khiron almost took a step back.

He studied her knowing that if he said no he would have to kill her and find another way of getting to Ray in a day's time. But he also knew that what she was asking for was a promise that he couldn't keep. Still he looked into her eyes and put on the most sincere face he could muster.

"You have my word ma," the lie burned on his tongue and he cupped her face. "I promise."

♟ CHAPTER 23

Ray stood in an all black suit watching Adrianna say her last goodbyes to Amann and D once they were in the Earth. Sadie, Devynn, and Mocha already said theirs and were in the backseat of the limousine that was waiting to take them all back to Ray's home. Although covered by a black lace veil he could still read the sadness drenched on her face. She wore a black Versace dress that stopped just below her knew and a pair of all black open toe Red Bottom four inch heels. Her lips, stained with lipstick the color of red wine, were pursed as she dropped the roses on their tombstones right beside each other. The deaths of two of their own hadn't really set until she saw them laying lifeless in their coffins. The coroner had done a good job, he'd made them look as if they were asleep. Buried like two bosses. They were in tuxedos and the collars covered their severed necks. The two of them came in the game together, so it was only right for them to leave the same way; just not like that. The way they were murdered was malicious and with no reasoning. She could have seen if they had started a war with another territory but truth was they were too busy making money to pay attention to the moves of the other cities unless they were on the come up. She knew it couldn't have been either of the six they had business with, but who?

"Whoever did this," Adrianna spoke when she felt Ray creep up behind her, "will burn. I put that on my life."

Ray nodded his head in agreement. Adrianna turned to Ray and looked at him through the veil on her face.

"They didn't deserve this!" She exclaimed tears forming in her eyes. "They were just supposed to be dropping off the money and coming back to meet us! When they didn't call I didn't trip because I thought they were with you and— I should have called or something fuck! How did this happen?"

Nothing hurt a boss more than losing his own to the unknown. Since the day Ray found out of their deaths. He had niggas on every block looking for anything that seemed *slightly* out of place. So far nothing. It was pissing him off to the point of no return that nobody had any info. He'd even contacted a few people in other cities, high and low, to see if anyone had any wind of a hit going down in Detroit. Nobody knew anything. He knew he had to grab the situation by its reigns before Vinny thought he was losing control of the city. Ray ran the city with power but also with love and it showed him love back. He knew that it couldn't have been anyone there who killed D or Amann.

"I got niggas on every block looking for unfamiliar faces ma," Ray told her. "I'm trying"

"Not hard enough!" Adrianna barked her accent thick. "Their blood should be streaming through the streets of the fuckin city, just like our brother's!"

"I can't dead a fuckin' ghost Adrianna!" Ray yelled back.

He had never raised his voice at a woman, but the truth was the fact that he had no leads and no idea of who committed the murders was eating away at him. He was supposed to be in tune with every happening in his city but somebody got him. He knew that whoever did it was bold, but not bold enough to come at him directly. Instead they went an even smarter route. Most niggas would want you to know the damage they caused, but whoever it was wanted Ray to be in a distraught position. He knew that much because it was what he would do and knowing that he knew he needed to clear his mind. Adrianna looked slightly taken aback and Ray instantly felt guilty.

"My bad ma," Ray said.

Adrianna and Ray never crossed the boundaries between business and work; it couldn't be denied that there was a spark. Ray had a soft spot for her and over the time of the Last King's take over it had often been tempting to make her wifey. She was everything he needed in a woman, nothing like the women he one nighted and sent on their way. She was the type of woman that would be a forever thing. But he knew it couldn't happen; just like she did. Ray respected her boss mentality and the fact that she never overstepped her boundaries. But right there in that moment the pain Ray saw on her face was almost unbearable. He pulled her into his wide chest and held her there. Adrianna clenched the back of Ray's suit jacket in her fists and buried her head in his long dreads. She could stay in his arms forever.

"Promise me that when you find out who did this," Adrianna whispered, "That you'll bled them dry."

Ray's face was atop of her soft hair but his eyes were on the graves. His little niggas deaths wouldn't be for nothing, he knew that.

"I promise."

The two separated and with one last farewell to their brothers they made their way to the waiting limousine.

"You ok ma?" Devynn asked Adrianna when she sat down next to her.

"No," Adrianna answered truthfully as the limo pulled off making its way to Ray's estate. "And I won't be until whoever did this is in a fuckin body bag."

Everyone but Mocha nodded in agreement. Instead she turned her head to look out the window.

"Where's Tyler?" Sadie asked her cousin hoping he knew.

She'd called him a few times since they parted ways after touching down back in Detroit but received no answer or call back. Before Jamaica she and Tyler didn't really talk like that, but she knew he wouldn't just automatically switch back into that mind state. Not after everything. She knew he was going to get Marie but no one had heard from her either of them. She was surprised Ray wasn't livid when he didn't show up for D and Amann's funeral but he said his man just didn't do funerals. That would be understandable. Had it not been for the fact that Sadie saw the look on his face when Devynn delivered the news. Something was wrong; she could feel it in her gut. Ray's phone rang before he could give her an answer.

"Hello...this is him," everyone in the back of the limo watched Ray's face drop even more than it was already had been. There was a long pause as he listened "He's alive? Ok. Thank you."

Sadie was too afraid to ask him what was just said over the phone once the call was disconnected.

"What happened Ray?" Devynn asked forcefully.

"They found Tyler's body this morning," Ray's lips moved but every other feature was frozen in place. "Six bullet holes; one to the head. They got him in an induced coma."

He sucked his lips in and nodded his head. His best friend and his right hand man. Whoever was behind the hits on the Last Kings had hit the wrong man. Sadie let out a small cry and tears filled her eyes.

"One by one their killing us off," Devynn spoke in a low tone. "Who the fuck is doing this shit?!"

No one spoke because no one had an answer. The only thought going through Sadie's mind was that she needed to get to the hospital Tyler was at. She needed to see Tyler. The fact that he was still alive said nothing about how much longer he had to live. Any thoughts of Marie and her whereabouts fled her mind, all she cared about was him.

"Get me to the hospital," she called to Pierre.

"No," Ray said forcefully. He was taking charge. "Pierre I want you to get Sadie Mocha and Devynn to my house. Adrianna you come with me to the hospital."

"No!" Sadie screamed. "Fuck that shit! I have to see him Ray. He needs me right now."

Adrianna looked into Sadie's tear stained longing eyes and knew what she'd known since the beginning for the Last Kings. She loved Tyler, more than anything. After losing two of the loves of her life she knew how unbearable the pain was and the fact that she never got to say goodbye pushed the knife even further into her heart. Sadie had that chance if Tyler didn't make it but she could tell that Ray's word was final.

"Sadie shut the fuck up and listen to me," Ray raised his voice at Sadie seeing her once again as his little cousin that he had to protect instead of his business partner. "That's three down! The safest place for all of you is my fuckin house. It's not negotiable."

Sadie knew she could argue and fight all she wanted but Ray would make sure she got out of the car at the house. She also knew that once there Devynn would be given orders to not let her leave. Her heart was breaking all over again. She didn't want to lose Tyler right when she got him.

"Please," she whispered to her cousin. She knew he didn't understand nor could she make him understand but she had to go to that hospital.

Even though Ray knew Sadie cared about Tyler his take on the matter at hand never altered. Niggas were going to war on him and he had to make sure the ones he had left on his team were taken care of.

"No," he said finally. "I'll see you when I leave the hospital."

When they got to Ray's estate he gave Sadie a hug and kissed her on the cheek. He did the same to Mocha but she pulled away slightly. Ray and Adrianna switched to his Hummer and prepared to be in route to the hospital.

"Dev make sure no one gets in...or out. All of your guns? Make sure the safety is off em. I got niggas at the gate armed and with orders to dead any unknown face. Be easy and I'm going to get at you in a minute."

Devynn nodded at her orders in the rounded driveway in front of Ray's huge brick estate. She looked back and saw Maria opening the door for Mocha and Sadie and turned back to him.

"You should let her go Ray," she told him. "She loves him."

Ray nodded.

"I know," he admitted.

He knew about everything. Ever since Sadie hit age eighteen he noticed her budding infatuation with his right hand man. He also noticed how Tyler's eyes lit up whenever Sadie entered the room. He had long since given them his blessing but he knew that it would be up to them if they wanted to pursue it any further. Tyler was the only man that would be able to handle Sadie and take care of her the way only a boss could. He was the only man Ray trusted with her heart. That knowledge was the main reason why he would not allow Sadie to go and see Tyler in the state he was in.

"I'll see you after I see what's up with my mans," Ray said and shook Devynn's hand like he would a nigga because that's how she preferred to be treated.

Devynn said one last goodbye to Adrianna and watched them drive away until they were completely out of sight.

♟ CHAPTER 24

After Maria made dinner and we all had eaten dinner. We all ventured off into separate parts of the house. Devynn tried to make small talk with me but Tyler was the only thing on my mind. I text Ray and told him to call me as soon as he got there with Tyler's stats and the doctors diagnostics. I lay posted in my window seat overlooking the view before I tired of that. I needed to take a long hot bath to ease my mind. Dropping my pistol on my dresser I headed for my bathroom. While running my bath water I heard the door to my room open and shut.

"You ok Say?" I heard the familiar voice of Mocha say.

I turned and looked at her and shook my head.

"Shit wasn't supposed to be like this Mo," I said still not able to believe D and Amann were gone even though I'd seen them both in caskets. "Kings don't die."

Mocha said nothing, she just came in and sat on the toilet.

"Niggas just popping up out of nowhere killing muhfuckas. We have never had bad business with anyone since the beginning Mo, you know this. Pussy niggas can't even show who they are. I swear on my soul for every bullet in Tyler's body I'ma put in that nigga's dick. On God," I was going on a rant; I had to let it all out. "Kings. Don't. Fucking. Die. D and Amann were kings nigga and that means they'll live on through me, you, shit all of us. Fuck the fuck shit, this shit ends tonight."

I finally took a breath and saw that Mocha sitting with her eyes closed. Her long hair fell in front of her face and her shoulders were hunched. She was shaking like she was crying but I saw no tears. I went over to her and held her knowing that she needed me.

"It's ok Mo, we're going to get these niggas," I said into her hair.

She nodded her head and pushed me off of her. She then stood up and began to walk out of the bathroom door. Her back to me she stopped in mid stride.

"I'm so sorry Say," she said and before I could ask her why she ran out of the room.

I stared at the bathroom door for a second before I closed it. No one was in their right state of mind at that point. But I knew one thing for sure was that we needed to get in it. We were all we had left and an army needed their generals to be strong. I refused to lose my fuckin' city. I checked my phone to see if I had any message from Ray but saw nothing so I knelt down to test the temperature of my water with my hand. Under me I heard a loud thud but I figured it was just Maria bustling around. I knew no one could ever make it past Ray's security. The door behind me opened and I heard Mocha reenter the bathroom.

"What did Maria drop Mo?" I asked her and no sooner were the words out of my mouth did I hear gun fire from downstairs.

I jumped up to reach for my pistol. I knew that whoever it was were there to try and finish the job that they started.

"Mocha—" I started as I swiveled around to tell her to follow me but the person standing behind me wasn't Mocha. My heart dropped as I recognized the man behind me and I dropped my gun.

"Not quite," the tall man said and smiled the evil smile I remembered like it was yesterday.

"N-no," I barely whispered. "You're dead!"

"Once again, not quite," the man said and before I could do or say anything else the butt of his gun came crashing into my temple causing me to fall and hit my head again on the edge of the tub.

I heard laughter and felt pain sear through my body just before everything went black.

♛ CHAPTER 25

Ray and Adrianna rushed through the hospital doors to get to the room Tyler was in. At first Ray was relieved to know that Tyler was still alive but once he saw him in his hospital bed grief overwhelmed him. He went and sat in the chair beside him and listened to the light beeps of the machine he was strapped into. Adrianna stood back allowing Ray time with his best friend. The top of Tyler's head was bandaged and so was the majority of his body. She knew only a true soldier could take six bullets and live to tell the tale; hopefully.

Ray clenched his fists while he looked over Tyler. His eyes were shut and he was resting peacefully. When he asked the doctor what was the extent of Tyler's head injury he received some good news. The bullet never penetrated his brain and they were able to remove it from where it was embedded in his skull. The bad news was that Ray didn't know how he was going to tell him that Marie was missing.

"I always said you were hardheaded fam," Ray shook his head at how fortunate Tyler was. He knew it was luck. No man would shoot another man that many times if he wasn't shooting to kill. "Don't trip though bro, I got niggas out looking for the muhfuckas who did this to you, D, and Amann. Nobody is going to eat until I got the muhfukckas' hearts in my hands!"

Adrianna listened to the words and felt the power in them. She was in tune with every word and went to Ray and clasped his hand in hers. Tyler must have felt them too because his eyebrows furrowed and he let out a low grown as he came out of his coma. His eyes opened a slit each as he tried to focus on them but couldn't and they shut once more. Ray thought he was out again but then Tyler's mouth moved like he was speaking but no words came out.

"Tyler," Adrianna said softly at Tyler's futile attempt to speak. "You need to rest, you have some pretty serious injuries."

Tyler ignored her and still tried to talk.

"Alanna," he kept repeating in a gurgled voice. "For Alanna."

"Alana?" Adrianna whispered to Ray. "Who's Alana?"

Ray shrugged and tried to listen more intently to what his mans was saying.

"Fram Atlanna," Tyler tried again eyes clenched shut.

"Fram Atlanna?" Ray repeated. "From Atlanta! Ty nigga what you saying man."

Ray hoped Tyler would be able to muster more and he leaned forward to ensure that he missed nothing. Tyler took a lot of deep breaths in between his words but what he had to say was important even though he was pushing himself and using all of his nonexistent energy.

"Took Marie. From Atlanta...business. Khiron," Tyler was able to get out before his monitor started going crazy and he started coughing up blood.

An array of doctors and nurses came in to tend to him. Ray and Adrianna were ushered from the room but Ray had heard all that he needed to hear. Khiron was behind all of it. He should have known remembering Khiron's last words to him. Ray knew he must have been holding Marie hostage or something, her body should have turned up already. But why? Marie had never been a part of their operation, Tyler made sure of that. But what Ray knew was that if she was indeed still alive her life was on a countdown and Ray had to find her before her time was up. One thing Ray should have kept in mind after the meeting with Khiron was never underestimate your opponents. Never.

Now that he knew it was Khiron. He thought back to the meeting at Amore. He kept seeing Khiron's eyes shift downwards. He thought that he was just observing his surroundings, but when he thought more in depth about it. From Khiron's seat he had the perfect view of the entrance to the underground club. Also as soon as Khiron left D and Amann made the drop off. If he was the one who set up the hit at Lace then that meant his people saw D and Amann remove the money being harbored there and *that* meant he watched them take it to Amore. Ray was sure Khiron was already mad about the whole denial of business thing which made Amann and D the perfect targets, their affiliation to the Last Kings branded proudly on their arms. Ray almost choked on his air while his thoughts spiraled inside of his head. How could have been so naïve? The nigga was coming at their necks. He wanted the city but he could only have it over Ray's dead body and Ray didn't plan on dying.

"I need to get to Amore," Ray said turning to walk down the long hallway in the hospital. "This nigga is dead, stay here with Tyler and keep me posted."

"Khiron...Khiron...Khiron!" Adrianna repeated to herself until she remembered where she'd heard that name from.

Before he went to Jamaica she remembered Tyler talking to somebody with that name from Atlanta and setting up a meeting with Ray. Ray didn't put him on so that was a reason to be bitter, but to start a war? There had to be more to it.

"Ray wait!" she yelled and ran after him. "Don't do anything stupid. Please."

Ray turned on his heels and looked down at her.

"This nigga is going to pay ma," Ray told her rage in his eyes. "Two of my bros are dead and this nigga is somewhere prancing around my muhfuckin city making his claim! I'ma show this nigga kings don't fuckin' die. Say it!"

"Kings don't die," she said up at him. "We live on forever. I'm coming with you Ray, you need me."

"Nah ma," Ray grabbed her hands. "Hold it down here for me aight?"

Before Adrianna could protest Ray's lips were on hers. Their tongues tasted each other for the first time and neither one wanted to let go. Their embrace was one so precious that when Ray finally let her go Adrianna had tears in her eyes.

"Promise me I'll see you again," Adrianna said.

Ray chuckled.

"I promise," he smiled down at her. "And when I come back you're going to have to pack your bags because we're going away for a while."

In light of everything going on Adrianna somehow reached inside and pulled a smile out.

"Here," she reached under her skirt and handed Ray her chrome 9 mm pistol. "I want one of my bullets in that muhfucka."

Ray nodded his hand and instead of saying goodbye he planted a kiss on her forehead and left her standing alone in the hallway. Adrianna then turned back to the hospital room that Tyler was in. She stayed outside of the room and looked in through the window watching the nurses get Tyler situated once more. His eyes opened for a brief second and locked on hers before they put him under once more. Her eyes fell on her Last King tattoo on her foot and she nodded her head.

"Hang in there Ty," she whispered. "Kings don't die."

Inside of her Chanel clutch she felt her cell phone vibrating. Seeing it was Devynn she answered it immediately.

"Hello?" She answered.

"So-somebody set us up!" Devynn choked into the phone.

"What? Where are you?!" Adrianna's heart froze over and she listened to Devynn cough into the phone.

"I got away but Mocha and Sadie were taken yo," Devynn struggled to get out. "Ray's guards turned A, them niggas set us up! They let the niggas walk right in."

Adrianna went into Spanish rant cursing everyone walking the Earth at that moment.

"Bitch English! They blasted Maria as soon as she opened the door and I was next," Devynn informed her. "If I ain't have on my vest I'd be dead too. Where's Ray? Let that nigga know his team ain't loyal no more."

Ray, Adrianna forgot all about him. She took off in the direction he'd gone phone still on her ear listening to Devynn.

"It was Khiron!" Adrianna told Devynn while looking frantically around the hospital for Ray. She hopped on the elevator to hopefully catch him in the parking lot.

"That nigga from Atlanta?" Devynn asked. "Fuck! I told Tyler not to welcome that bitch into the city!"

Adrianna finally reached the hospital parking lot but had no luck in finding Ray.

"Shit!" She yelled out. "Where are you at Dev?"

"I took one of Ray's cars. I'm on my way to the hospital. Almost there now."

"I'm in the parking lot. Hurry up, we have to get to Amore!"

♟ CHAPTER 26

The sound of static aroused me. My eyes opened and everything around me was a blur. I could slightly see a TV on, but nothing was on the screen but a piece of paper. I didn't move until my vision came in all the way and when it did I noticed all familiar surroundings. I was laying down on a soft twin bed in a tank to and a pair of shorts. There was no light on in the room but a little ray beamed through a window above my head. Looking around I saw all of my stuffed animals atop a chestnut dresser. It was a sight I saw everyday in the morning when I woke up at…Grandma Rae's house! I jumped out of the bed but was floored almost the same exact second. The pain I felt in my head was unbearable but I still crawled to the bedroom door. There was light seeping into the room from under the door but I saw no shadows or heard no form of life. I struggled to my feet and tried to snatch the door open. No luck. The door was locked from the other side.

"What's happening?" I said aloud to myself backing away from the door. "Grandma Rae? Grandma Rae!" I called.

As I backed away from the door my foot got caught on something and I fell backwards with a loud thud. My hands felt around for the cause of my fall and I shuddered when they found what they were looking. I did something I didn't know I was capable of doing. I screamed. I screamed a spine tingling scream because my hands recognized the cold clammy face they were placed on. Eyes, lips, and nose...when my hands reached the familiar texture of hair and felt that the back of the head was completely gone I broke down.

"No! No! No!" I cried and clutched my grandmother's stiff body and cried. "I'm so sorry Grandma Rae. I love you, I'm so sorry!"

I didn't care that her body was cold and lifeless or that I was lying in a pool of blood for that matter. I lay there for what seemed like forever crying. When I finally did look up my eyes, blurry once again that time from crying, fell on the television. I didn't notice until then that there was a note stuck to it. Arms shaking I let my grandma's body go and stood to my feet. I flipped on the light switch in the room but instantly wished I hadn't. Blood was splattered all over the wall in my old room letting me know it was where my grandmother's murder was committed. I looked down at my clothes and saw blood there too. I'd seen many dead bodies in the past year, I helped at to them, but seeing my grandmother's body brought on a strong urge to vomit. My heart broke inside of my chest and I couldn't do anything but turn my head towards the television. I took a deep breath and stepped over Grandma Rae's body. I crept to the television keeping an eye on the door half expecting whoever was keeping me there to burst through and kill me next. No one did. I snatched the note off of the TV screen. I unfolded it and looked blankly at the tiny words staring back at me.

Press Play.

I glanced up at the VCR that sat atop television and saw that a little green light was shining indicating that it was powered on. Trembling at what I was about to witness my finger found its way to the play button and applied a tiny amount of pressure. The screen changed from static to footage of a bedroom. The camera appeared to be perched on someone's bedroom dresser pointing at a king sized bed. The lights in the room were dimmed but there was something vaguely familiar about the room. My stomach was slowly dropping as I tried to make sense of what I was seeing on the screen. The room was clearly a large one but I could only see what the camera showed me. I couldn't see the door to the room but I heard it open and shut. What I heard next was enough to twist my falling stomach into knots.

"Please stop! I don't want it," a young girl's voice pleaded.

She began backing up unknowingly into the view of the camera wearing only a night gown. Her complexion was of a brown skinned complexion. Her hair long and straight sat disheveled on her head. She was average height and although she had the curves of a grown woman she couldn't have been more than fourteen. She turned facing the camera as a man entered the view as well. The sharpness in her eyes was clouded by the tears dripping down the high cheekbones on her pretty face. I gasped as I stared at myself in disbelief. Floored at the sickening realization that Nino had filmed the things he did to me…and I never knew.

It was like reliving a nightmare…I didn't feel as if I were watching it I felt like I was there all over again…

"Nino please don't!" I begged my mother's man in a meek voice. "I do everything you ask me to. Just don't hurt me anymore."

I backed up until I stumbled backwards on my king sized bed. I knew pleading with him would do nothing just by seeing the hungry look in his eyes. He would still take my womanhood, something I never gave willingly, just like he did every other night.

"Nah..." Nino licked his lips while parting my thighs. "That pussy is too tight to pass up."

"But you promised Nino! You promised! You said if I put in more work than your best trapper you would stop!"

I was sobbing by then just at the mere thought of the broken promise. The promise was what drove me to hustle harder than any nigga Nino had patrolling the streets. In one month I single handedly racked in a little over twenty racks. I should have known the man who had the gumption enough to stick his dick inside his lady's fourteen year old daughter wouldn't keep his word. Nino began laughing, showing his pearly whites. Women went crazy over Nino but his gorgeous outer layer was out shined by the evil content of his heart.

"Mom," I whispered as he loomed over me unstrapping his belt and dropping his pants.

"Your mom is somewhere in this fuckin' house passed out lil shorty. She ain't worried about you," he dropped to his knees grinning at the sight of my fat lips under my night gown. "Damn I guess it's true what they say. Like mother, like daughter."

Nino roughly finished parting my legs as I lay there just staring at the ceiling wishing I was anywhere but there. I braced myself for the feeling of disgust soon to come. My tears were warm as they rolled freely down my temples into my hair. I closed my eyes and tried to enter a world where no one could hurt me. Nino tore my panties off and lifted my gown just enough so my bottom half was completely visible to the world.

"I'm about to give you your first squirting orgasm," he whispered and began slowly massaging my engorged clitoris with his thumb.

Don't get wet, don't get wet. I thought but my body didn't pay me any mind, my vagina had a mind of its own and I could feel my juices start flowing.

I hated Nino. I hated my hate for Nino. Over the period of time that he'd been raping me he took an even more twisted take on the matter. He didn't want me to fight it, instead he made it his job to find each and every way to give me pleasure. He'd made me come more times than I could count and I despised myself for it. With every blissful feeling and every drop of juice dripping from in between my thighs I dies a little bit more inside.

"Yea," Nino whispered to me still working his thumb. "You know you like this shit girl. Go 'head and make that pussy soak for Daddy's dick."

Nino watched in amazement at how wet I was becoming and I clenched my eyes shut refusing to enjoy the malicious act being committed against my womanhood. Where was my mother? She knew what Nino did to me she should be there stopping him! Instead she got high. So she couldn't hear my screams for help. She'd thrown me under the bus for the man that supported her habit and I couldn't help but to love her.

Nino's tongue caught me by surprise and my body jerked. His tongue was beating my clit like a drum and it took every ounce of self control I had left not to moan. Instead I sobbed louder. I cried as he devoured my tender spot because it felt so good and I knew it was wrong. His hands gripped my thighs tightly while he flicked his hot tongue in and out of me. When he was done he smacked his lips like he'd just finished a full course meal and stood up. His erection pointed straight out making his boxers look like a tent. He smiled sinisterly down at me and I cringed knowing what was about to happen next. He dropped his boxers and began stroking his beast. His dick was big, nine inches long and at least three inches wide, and I often wondered why he wanted me. He could have any woman he desired but yet he was in my bedroom every night.

"You ready baby?" he spoke to me like his lover, not a child.

He lifted my nightgown over my head exposing my already full breasts. His hands each palmed one and his fingers skillfully massaged the tips of my engorged nipples.

"I hate you," I whispered.

My tears stopped flowing as I accepted my fate just like every other time. His hands were soft on my skin, but I flinched with every touch. The tips of his fingers trailed down my body until they rested on my hips, gripping them as he prepared to enter me raw. Nino put me on birth control when he first started fucking me to ensure that I didn't get pregnant. He hated condoms and he also had a fetish for nutting in my "young pussy." Leaving his mark.

"You hate me?" He asked and slid all nine inches inside of me without a warning.

The thrust was powerful and awakened every sensation my walls had causing them to clench tightly around his shaft. My back arched and I clenched my eyes shut at the pain. He thrust again..and again. Until the pain subsided only to be replaced by a pleasure so strong I had to bit my lip. Nino placed his mouth by my ear and began whispering things. He told me how beautiful I was and how good it felt inside of me.

"You're so beautiful shorty," he said over and over as he hit it harder with every stroke. "This shit is dripping ma!"

I tried to keep my hands limp at my sides while he defiled my body, but soon they were gripping his shoulders as he rode me to ecstasy.

Sadie no, I thought. Don't like it. Don't like—

"Ahh!" I moaned loudly into his ear when he used his fingers to roughly pinch my right nipple.

He was diving in so deep, every thrust thumped my love box, soon it was going to burst.

"This is my pussy," he panted into my ear. "You hear me girl? You belong to me! Fuuck! This shit is tight."

When it came to Nino it was a hit and miss. Some nights he was rough and abusive. Other nights he was sweet and sensual like a boyfriend. But he wasn't, he was a rapist. I despised the fact that I was enjoying it. My hips began throwing it at him matching him stroke for stroke.

"Yea I knew you liked this shit girl! Throw it up at daddy!"

My pussy liked it, I didn't. My mind was screaming to stop but my body was saying keep going. When I felt my orgasm coming I tried my hardest to stop it, but that made it come even harder. I screamed and my eyes rolled to the back of my head. It felt like I was peeing but I knew I wasn't. Nino pumped three more times before pulling his penis out with his hand and squirting his cum all over my face and hair.

"You ain't shit bitch," he said coldly standing over me. "You ain't never going to be shit either. If I tell you to get out there and trap, that's what the fuck you're going to do. If I want some pussy you're going to part them legs for daddy. I own you bitch. You and your momma, and if you don't do what I say I will blow ya fucking heads off."

I turned my head from the scene being played on the television. I couldn't bare to watch anymore. I couldn't watch the younger tortured me tremble any longer. Whoever had taken me knew about my past...Nino? It couldn't have been. The Italians murdered him. My heart was beating hard and I was panicking. Although fear was present in my heart anger was too. Without thinking pushed the TV off of the desk that it was placed on. There was a loud crash and glass covered the floor. I snatched the VCR up and flung it against the wall shattering it into a dozen pieces.

"Fuck you!" I screamed to my capers fists balled.

I was becoming hysterical. I didn't know how long I'd been passed out and I wasn't going to be contained like a fucking animal for some sick pervert's entertainment. I wondered if Ray knew I was missing, what if he didn't? I wasn't strapped, I was defenseless. Under the door I saw a shadow moving and heard footsteps. I looked around my room for anything to defend myself with and came up short. Keys jingled and I heard the lock on the door click allowing whoever was on the other side entrance. The door slowly opened until the gape was wide enough to step through. The person who stepped through was very handsome, dressed in regular street clothes and the resemblance between him and the demon from my past was uncanny. I couldn't help it, I took a few steps back away from him. My knees buckled and I felt like the helpless fourteen year old girl I once was.

"N-Nino?" I asked not believing my eyes.

His curls sat atop of my captor's head perfectly just like Nino's. The skin complexion all the way down to the way he stood was Nino. The man smiled at me and shook his head.

"Nah ma," he stepped closer and I focused my eyes realizing that it wasn't the man from my nightmares after all. The man began walking towards me, stepping over Grandma Rae's dead body. "My name is Khiron, not that it matters."

"Khiron?" I asked confused.

That was the name of the nigga Tyler set up to meet with Ray. But why?

"I've been waiting for this moment for a *long* time Sadie," he said soflty as he advanced on me. I saw the butt of his pistol poking through his muscle shirt so I knew rushing him would be the move of a dumb bitch.

"When Ray finds out—" I started but was cut off by loud laughter.

"Not even Ray can save you now bitch. I've been waiting for this shit for six fuckin' years!"

Khiron looked down at the broken television and the glass from the screen that was scattered on the bloodstained carpet. He stopped an arm's length in front of me with his head cocked.

"What...you didn't like my little home movie? Or should I say *your* little home movie," he chuckled "Damn shorty you was a freak though. I can see why Nino kept biting."

The knots in my stomach tightened. My past, something that I thought was over, had finally caught up to me. I knew he was the one behind all of the havoc being caused in the city but none of it added up. Ray denied business with him, so the fuck what, that couldn't have been it.

"Why are you doing this?" I cut my eyes at him. "Ray is going to kill you."

"Ray doesn't even know what the fuck is going on bitch. How can you call yourself a boss and don't even know what the fuck is going on in your own city? He ain't shit but a fuck nigga but he's just icing on the cake. You Sadie? You're the big fish I've been wanting. It was one hell of a coincidence too! When that bitch ass nigga told me I couldn't hold his product I was going to just chill. But then I found out he worked with the Italians; I couldn't just leave. Not without taking what's rightfully mine"

"What the fuck are you talking about?!" I yelled into his face. "And how did you get those tapes?"

The house burned down. I saw it. There was no way anything could have been preserved ...least of all

Nino's sick fetish tapes. Who the fuck was that nigga and how did he know about my past? Khiron's cold stare turned distant and foggy.

"You were all he ever talked about. He always told me how hustle lived in your heart…and how much of a waste it was on a little bitch like you," Khiron was talking and my mind was reaching trying to grasp his words. "Imagine my frustration. Being in the shadow of someone I never even met! I was nineteen and on the verge of inheriting an empire bigger than you could ever dream! But because of you I was held back from it because somehow you could put in more work than me. That made me…" Khiron paused and snapped his fingers. "Now what was the word he used? Awh yea that's right *incompetent.*"

Without warning he struck me once in my face so hard I felt my jaw crack. I fell to the ground with a large thud and he walked up and kicked me hard in my ribs. I felt blood evade my mouth and I spit it out clutching my stomach where I lay. Khiron began pacing back and forth in front of me and he continued with his story.

"Bitch! I remember the last time he came to visit me. It was the weekend. Summer vacation just started and he was meeting with an Italian connect in Atlanta, but something was wrong with him. The nigga was jumpy and a boss is never jumpy. When he left it was in a hurry and he forgot his duffle bag. I called it his duffle bag of secrets. He never even said goodbye."

He stopped pacing and knelt down in front of my aching face. I was confused, why would Khiron care about a goodbye from another nigga? I struggled to sit up to face, mind reeling. I thought back to Nino's monthly trips to Atlanta. I knew he went there because he ran big business there but he also went there to visit... Something in my mind clicked and my heart froze over.

"You're his son," I whispered wide eyed. "You're Nino's son."

I couldn't believe how naïve I'd been. The resemblance between Khiron and Nino was undeniable. Nino always called Khiron "Khy" when he spoke about him so I never knew his full name...I did now though. Khiron's distant look was replaced with coldness once again and he grabbed me by my hair. He studied my face.

"Finding out my pops had a thing for young pussy was a little disturbing. That shit was sick especially since he was still fuckin' my mom, but I still watched the tapes," he yanked my head so that his mouth was directly on my ear and spoke in a soft taunting tone. "I watched you beg and scream and cry over and over. He had cameras in his office too Sadie..."

His voice trailed off and echoed in my head.

No, I thought shaking my head knowing what he was saying.

My mind took me back to the day I'd broken into Nino's office. I was so clouded with anger that day six years ago that I'd been careless. I never would have thought Nino would be sick enough to record the malicious acts he did with me, but I should have known that his office was under surveillance. Khiron let go of my hair and leaned back to get a good look at the expression on my face.

"Priceless," he said. "Yea bitch I knew it was you who had my pops killed. Snitch! You killed everything bitch!"

Khiron kicked me again and more blood came up. I knew that unless some sort of miracle happened I was going to be murdered in that basement. I never in a million years thought that the son of the man I had killed would come out looking to spill blood. I felt tears rush to my eyes as the reality hit me. It was my fault D and Amann were dead. Khiron was toying with me, he was enjoying seeing me suffer.

"Where's Mocha?" I asked with a mouth full of salty blood. "And Devynn?"

"Devynn is dead, bitch took a shot gun shell to the chest," Khiron laughed and tears came to my eyes.

Devynn and I weren't the closest but she was a real bitch and a true soldier. She didn't deserve to die.

"You bitch!" I screamed. "They didn't do anything to you! Why did you kill them!"

"All of you have to die," Khiron shrugged. "I'm taking Detroit, fuck a business deal."

"No!" I yelled. "Where's Mocha?"

I was afraid of what he was going to say, I would take his gun and dead myself if he told me she'd met the same fate as Devynn.

"Don't trip shorty," Khiron said his Georgia drawl strong. "That bitch is probably on a yacht chilling eating crab cakes or some shit."

"Stop lyin' nigga! Where is she?" I snarled rushing him only to receive a blow harder than the first one.

"It's funny that you're worried about ya homegirl when she's the one who gave up your whereabouts.

She's the one who brought me here to grandma's house, who I might add was one feisty old bitch. You wanna know where she is?"

Khiron came to where my body was laid out next to Grandma Rae's and once again grabbed the back of my tussled hair forcing my head up to look at him. All three of him. As my eyes tried to focus on his face I heard somebody else enter the room.

"You wanna know where she is Sadie?" Khiron yelled pulling my hair so hard I felt some rip away from my scalp.

"Yes," I said weakly cringing in pain.

"I'm right here," a voice so familiar to me said.

I didn't want to believe the owner of the voice was my ride or die bitch. My day one. But when my eyes averted to the figure standing in the door way I knew it was real. My vision was blurry and my mind slightly out of it but I could spot Mocha from a mile away. She was my best friend; was. The betrayal I felt was so powerful it hurt physically. The hurt I felt overpowered the anger. Mocha stood over me bleeding in a mixture of my own and Grandma Rae's blood in a designer dress and open toe stilettos. She looked like a celebrity. Khiron threw my head back down viciously almost causing me to blackout again before standing up. Through my clouded vision I watched him walk to Mocha and kiss her sloppily on her mouth. She let him for a second but then she pushed him off of her.

"This isn't how it was supposed to happen Khiron!" I could hear in her voice that she was starting to cry. "You promised me you wouldn't hurt her!"

Khiron laughed.

"Baby I'm a dope man, that was your mistake if you believed me. This is what I do. If you have a problem you can join this bitch in the afterlife," Khiron told her. When she was quiet he continued. "This bitch killed my pops! This is the bitch responsible for taking *my* empire baby! Awh yea I'm killing this bitch!"

I used all of my strength to sit up and stare into Mocha's eyes. A huge knot was forming on the right side of my face but I ignored the screeching pain.

"Why Mocha?" I asked. "Why would you turn on us?"

"I-I love him Sadie," Mocha said what only a weak bitch would and shrugged her shoulders meekly. "He promised me a life outside of the drug ring. A life of riches without having to put in any work, you know that's all I ever wanted! This was your dream Say! Not mine!"

"You could have had that Mocha!" I screamed letting the tears fall. "At any fucking time! I would have had you! You let this snake ass nigga know where we laid our heads, for what? So you could go shopping all day and sit at home?! You're going to let him take everything for your own selfishness. Fuck you Mocha when he kills me don't even mourn my death because you're already dead to me."

Mocha's eyes went wide at my words and a sob escaped her mouth.

"All those trips to Atlanta," I shook my head at how dumb I'd been to trust her. That's how she met Khiron, she was his key to me.

I stared at Mocha disgusted that she'd chosen dick over me. She was like my sister, blood couldn't have made us any closer. I trusted her with everything I had and there she was staring down at me in my demise. She looked at Grandma Rae and turned her head so she couldn't see her until she stepped over her to get to me. She dropped on her knees and grasped my hands.

"It wasn't supposed to be like this Say," her lips trembled when she spoke. "I'm sorry."

I pulled my hands from hers and spat in her face.

"Fuck you," I said and meant it.

Mocha stared into my eyes for a few more moments and I saw her heart break. I knew she saw mine break too.

"No," she shook her head and stood up and ran up on Khiron swinging her fists. "You're not going to kill her! We had a deal!"

"It's too late Mocha!" Khiron grabbed her and threw her hard to the side. He pulled his .45 from his waste and advanced on me again. "You're going to live and watch what you caused, you won't get the luxury of death."

He aimed the chrome barrel at me and fired once catching me in my leg. I'd never been shot before and the pain was excruciating but I didn't scream. I fell back and tried to stomach the pain."No Khiron!" I heard Mocha scream and a bullet hole appeared inches away from my head.

"Get off me!" Khiron said and I heard another thud and a grunt from Mocha.

I turned my head in time to see Khiron coming for me and I tried to get up but the pressure from Khiron's foot on my chest prevented that from being possible. So I laughed. I laughed like a crazed person and I saw the look of confusion on his face. I was about to die, I knew it but my mouth still worked perfectly fine.

"You think you can kill me bitch!" I said through clenched teeth. "Kings. Don't. Fucking. Die!! You will never be near as much of a boss as me. Even your punk ass daddy knew that! Fuck that nigga too I'm glad I had that nigga killed, and guess what? No matter what happens in this basement…you'll be next!"

The pressure of Khiron's foot lessened and he stared down at me as I laughed. His lip up turned and he aimed his gun at my heart.

"You took everything from me, so I'm going to do the same thing to you. You're going to burn. And Ray? I'm about to kill him too."

I saw Khiron's jaw clench just before he pulled the trigger twice more and I felt heat in my chest and in my stomach.

"R-Ray," was all I could get out before I began choking on my own blood.

"N-n-nooooo!!!" Mocha screamed and tried to get to me.

Khiron strong armed her and held her back. He grinned at me enjoying the sight of me dying slowly. The world around me was becoming dim and I knew my life that remained on the earth was short. I coughed on the blood that spilled from my mouth and the pain in my chest was unbearable. My hands clutched my stomach trying to catch the blood, but there was so much of it and it was no use. I just wanted the pain to stop.

"Sadie I'm so sorry!" Mocha screamed. "Why?! No! No! No!"

Her voice grew distant and my eyes closed The pain was slowly subsiding and my last thought before everything went black was Grandma Rae's voice.

"Sadie you're my special baby. You have a special heart, you hear? You're going to do great things in this world. My special girl, you make this world. Don't you let it make you.

I let go of the little piece of life I was holding on to in sorrow with sadness and comfort that soon Ray would be joining me.

Chapter 27

Ray entered Amore and immediately knew something was up. It was empty. Top and bottom levels. No one was there, not even his workers. It was so quiet he would have been able to hear a pin drop. Gun raised he went to the secret entrance of the club that was in the basement and found where all of his workers were. They were all sprawled out on the floor dead, his money and product on the ground around them.

"Ray," he heard a voice whisper behind him and as soon as he turned around to click on the owner something hit him in the head so hard and he fell to the ground blacked out.

When Ray finally opened his eyes it felt as if no time had passed but his body felt different. He looked around and the dead bodies of his employees let him know he was still in the same place. But when he tried to move his body he found he couldn't. Looking down he saw that he was bound tightly to a chair and no matter how hard he tried to fight against them he couldn't get free. Around him he saw that he was circled in by a group of men. He recognized none of their faces nor did he see a Last King tattoo anywhere on their bodies.

"There's no point fam," Ray heard a vaguely familiar voce say. "You ain't getting' free."

Ray's head whipped around looking for the source of the voice, but with his head injury that just made him dizzy.

"Who the fuck is there?" he called out angry that he'd been caught slipping.

"I told you I'd be seeing you Ray," the voice said. "You know who the fuck it is."

Ray heard footsteps behind him until a man appeared in front of him. Khiron stood over him like a man gloating over a big fish that he'd just caught. And that's exactly what Ray was.

"I'm not going to make this last too long, I've already gotten what I wanted," Khiron smiled evilly at Ray. "This shit was too easy; easier than I expected. Glad you waited until I got here to come back to your senses. This should be fun."

He laughed out loud and looked above Ray for a split second.

"You have a really nice house by the way," he taunted. "I burned it down of course."

Ray fought harder against the rope around his wrists and ankles but only tired himself. Sadie was in that house, if he'd burned it down with her in it…

"Don't worry," Khiron chuckled pulling up a chair in front of Ray and taking a seat. "She was alive when we left the house."

The sick smile he wore like a shirt gave Ray a queasy feeling.

"Where are they?" Ray growled in a low voice. His tone was deadly. "Where are Mocha, Devynn and Sadie?"

"Devynn is dead, I had no use for that bitch," Khiron shrugged his smile still planted on his face. "And Mocha? Well see for yourself. Mocha!"

Mocha then too appeared in front of Ray confusing him and when he saw the tears in her eyes he knew something was wrong.

"I'm so sorry Ray," she whispered.

"Tell him where Sadie is Mocha," Khiron grabbed Mocha and pulled her so that she was sitting on his lap looking directly at Ray. "Tell him about how you gave me the directions to his home. Tell him about how you brought me to his grandmother's house and how I blew her fuckin' head off. Tell him about how you watched me put the bullet in her heart."

Mocha was shaking as she stared into Ray's eyes and watched him fight against his restraints at the news he'd just received. That was the only time that she'd ever seen him look any form of weak. He'd always been their rock, their savior. He stopped fighting after a while and looked tired and beat. His dreads hung loosely around his slumped shoulders and his eyes instantly were filled with pain at Khiron's words. He knew they were true by the tears rolling down Mocha's face and the sobs she was choking on. Ray was about to speak but he had no words to say. He looked around at his establishment and the thousands of dollars on the ground and shook his head. His eyes fell on the entrance of the club and he saw Devynn and Adrianna's faces. Devynn had her guns out ready to rain fire on them all but he shook his head slightly. If they entered the room they would surely be dead, especially since Khiron already thought Devynn was. He saw tears form in Adrianna's eyes and he thought of his promise to her. Promises in his eyes were never meant to be broken, especially if it was made by him. But at that moment he knew that was the only promise he made in his life that he wouldn't be able to keep.

"You shot her in her heart?" Ray turned his attention back to Khiron. "In my grandmother's house?"

He was trying to send Devynn and Adrianna a subliminal message. Get to that house. Saving him was a lost cause unless they all wanted to die together. His eyes averted back to Mocha and he spat on her in disgust.

"I took you in because of your loyalty to my cousin. You both better hope that whatever bullet enters my body kills me or may God have mercy on ya fucking souls…because I won't. And I *know* she won't."

Khiron laughed at the man before him ignoring his comment.

"I thought about shooting you, but that's so old fashioned. Don't you think my nigga?" Khiron pushed Mocha off of his lap and one of the men surrounding them grabbed her by her arm to retrain her just in case she got out of control. "I want to watch you scream. I brought down the best! The Italians are going to have to find another flunky bitch, look up."

Ray did as he was told and looked at what Khiron had glanced at earlier. Hanging from the ceiling was a huge bucket and a rope was attached to it. Ray's eyes followed the rope and saw that one of Khiron's goons was holding the other end of it an evil glint in his eyes.

"Acid," Khiron stood up and backed away. "There won't even be a skeleton when we're finished here."

"No! Please Khiron don't!" Mocha begged trying to fight against the man holding her.

Ray's eyes locked on Adrianna's and he smiled. They would never know what could have been...what should have been. Adrianna covered her mouth when Khiron gave the man the signal to let go of the rope and turned her head into Devynn's shoulder just before the liquid hit Ray's body. There was a spine tingling scream, but it belonged to Mocha not Ray. He wasn't going to give Khiron the satisfaction. He felt his body disintegrate and gave in to death before his entire body was no more. It didn't take long for the acid to eat away at his flesh and when Adrianna looked again she saw bones falling apart as the acid still ate away at them. Ray was no more, it felt like her heart had been ripped out of her chest and thrown into the acid that killed him.

"And that ladies and gentlemen," Khiron whispered just loud enough to be heard. "Is how you take over an empire."

♟EPILOGUE

"Sadie?" I stared at the woman I'd believed was dead for a year in disbelief.

The eyes of my former best friend had changed. There was emptiness there. Although my gun was in my hand I was too petrified to pull it on her. I felt like I was looking into the eye of a ghost.

"H-How?" I saw her die. I *saw* Khiron kill her! "What?" Sadie said her voice soft and cold as she cocked her head slightly at me. "You want a fuckin' hug? What's the matter Mo, you look like you just saw a ghost!"

There was something different in her demeanor. The golden pharaoh on her forearm glistened in the night indicated who her allegiance was still and would forever be with.

"Sadie I'm so sorry," I spoke the same words to her flesh right then and there that I thought her spirit was hearing every night. "I never wanted any of that to happen, it wasn't supposed to be like that."

I felt tears welling up in my eyes as I stared into the blankness in hers. The expression on her face let me know that she could care less about my words, they meant nothing to her. I noticed the black gloves on her hands and instantly knew why she was there. I let my grip loosen on Lucy. The remorse I felt for the fall of the Last Kings was unbearable. It was six cartels in one and because of me it was over. Instead the only work that was seen in Detroit was the weak shit Khiron had going. Sadie's gaze waivered and for a split second I saw the rage that was held inside.

"You want to know how I survived huh?" Sadie chuckled. "You should have paid more attention to Grandma Rae. I have a special heart Mocha...you remember her saying that?"

I nodded my head, she said it everyday but I didn't see how it was relevant.

"The bullet Khiron put in my chest didn't penetrate it. My heart is on the opposite side of my chest unlike the common person. That's what she meant by saying my heart was special, I found that out after the fact of being shot. If Khiron was smart he would have put more than two bullets in my body; his mistake. But then again if it hadn't been for Adrianna and Devynn showing up when they did I would have been dead no question. It took six months of physical therapy and being connected to fuckin' tubes to fully function again."

Distantly I remembered Ray's last words

"May God have mercy on ya fucking souls...because I won't. And I know she won't."

"Did it make you happy?" Sadie asked me calmly. "Watching Ray die?"

All I could do was let the tears roll down my face and shake my head.

"We took you in Mocha!" Sadie's eyes ripped me into shreds. "Bitch you didn't have one person to live for and we gave you that! But then you choose a nigga over us? Over family? I don't have anybody now Mocha. Not Grandma Rae, not Ray. Nobody!" Sadie began walking towards me a fire burning in her eyes. "My cousin couldn't even receive a proper burial because there was nothing left to bury. And for what? For this?"

Sadie waived her arms around the neighborhood as her heels stabbed the ground with each step she took.

"Bitch this nigga got you living out of a fuckin' shoebox hoeing on the low," Sadie shook her head in pity. "I could dead your ass, and trust me it's *so* tempting, but I'm not going to."

My mouth opened not understanding. If I was her I wouldn't even be having a conversation with me. I would have just put a bullet in my brain.

"I can't kill you actually," Sadie smirked at me. "Just like Khiron used you as his key, I'm using you as mine. And I need you to lead me to someone."

"Y-your key to what? And lead you to who?" I found my voice again.

"Kings don't fucking die, remember Mocha," Sadie was directly in front of my face. "And there's a peasant running my fucking city. I need it back. Marie's missing, I know she's not dead. Tyler isn't going to rest until he finds her."

She nodded down the street and I noticed an all black Hummer, Ray's bullet proof Hummer posted.

"Tyler's alive?" I breathed not believing it, I'd seen his obituary in the newspaper.

"You're not stupid Mocha you know what's up, we had to keep a low profile. But now it's time to take back what's ours, and you're going to help," Sadie turned her back on me and began to walk away but then stopped and turned her head slightly. "This meeting? It never happened. The real war starts tomorrow. Play your role, you'll be hearing from me soon. Oh and don't worry if this doesn't work I *will* kill you, then shoot Khiron's mother's house up and make him come look for me."

With that I watched Sadie switch back to the Hummer and pull off into the night. Although she'd just threatened my life just the mere sight of her gave me hope. I knew I was going to do everything in my power to help her claim back the city; for Ray.

"Kings don't fucking die," I whispered up to the stars before I went inside of my shoebox to prepare for the street war to come.

TO BE CONTINUED...

Official Writer's League
ORDER FORM

$14.99

$14.99

$14.99

COMING SOON

COMING SOON

COMING SOON

COMING SOON

COMING SOON

COMING SOON

COMING SOON

COMING SOON

COMING SOON

COMING SOON

Wholesale orders: $6.75 + shipping (Minimum of 20 books)
Inmate Orders: $12.00 + Free shipping
Book Club Orders (minimum order of 10 books): $12.75 + shipping

WHOLESALE ORDERS CAN BE PLACED AT OWLBOOKORDERS@HOTMAIL.COM

TITLE	QTY
TOTAL	

NAME _____
(Include Prison #)

SHIP TO_____

MAIL FORM TO:
OWL Book Orders
PO Box 181048
Utica, MI 48318